L A

PASHLER'S LANE

Elizabeth Holdgate enjoyed a secure childhood in the little country town of Clare, Suffolk in the 1930s, and this is her tribute to the community which gave her so much. Pashler's Lane is named for her grandfather Freddie Pashler, dispenser of local warmth and wisdom, whose baker's shop used to flank it on Market Hill. He and other local 'characters' are seen here through a child's eyes as, between Priory and Common, Castle and Church the life of a self-sufficient little community rolled on, untouched (or so it seemed) by great events, until war came.

PASHLER'S LANE

268

PASHLER'S LANE

by

Elizabeth Holdgate

Dales Large Print Books
Long Preston, North Yorkshire,
BD23 4ND, England.

British Library Cataloguing in Publication Data.

Holdgate, Elizabeth
    Pashler's Lane.

    A catalogue record of this book is
    available from the British Library

    ISBN   978-1-84262-501-9 pbk

First published in Great Britain in 2002 by Fell Beck Press

Cover illustration © Melvyn Warren-Smith by arrangement with P.W.A. International Ltd.

Published in Large Print 2007 by arrangement with
Hayloft Publishing Ltd.

Dales Large Print is an imprint of Library Magna Books Ltd.

Printed and bound in Great Britain by
T.J. (International) Ltd., Cornwall, PL28 8RW

A NOTE ON THE TITLE

If you go to Clare today, you will find a little lane named 'Pashler's Alley'. It runs from the High Street to the Market Hill, and there is still a butcher's shop on one side of it, at the Market Hill end. But Grandad's shop – the baker's that was once opposite the butcher's – now sells motor parts and is unrecognizable. Yet Grandad is still there, for he of course is the Pashler of Pashler's Alley. In our time, though, it was 'the Lane', and in memory of that fact, and because I prefer Lanes to Alleys, I have re-named it as the title of this book.

ACKNOWLEDGMENT

My thanks go to my husband, Martin, for his never-failing support and encouragement and to Robert for using his desk-top publishing skill to produce a first version of this book.

To my mother, Edith Dickason,
with love and thankfulness
And for Katherine and Michael

Contents

A Snapshot of Clare

Clare was more than a village, yet less than a town, with two bakers, two blacksmiths, three shoe-shops, a large flint church with a too-short tower, two chapels (one Congregational and one Baptist), a Gas Works and at least ten public houses. It was a busy little place in those days, for it also had a Post Office, two Banks (both on the Market Hill), a well-stocked ironmonger's and a bevy of little shops that provided anything you could possibly think of needing. There was even a gentleman's outfitters which sold sturdy rainproofs and tweeds, where you could have a suit made by Arthur the tailor from Cavendish. For more exotic wants a bus would take you to Haverhill, Sudbury and even Bury St Edmunds on certain days of the week, but such journeys were few and far between, I believe. Occasionally, Grandad would go to Bury to visit his brother Herbert, another baker, and bring home a pint of tasty winkles, or even a pink-and-black crab which Mother attacked with a hammer and nutcrackers, and which was even more delicious.

From a tall castle mound and an Augustinian Priory by the River Stour to the south, Clare stretched northwards rather in the shape of a boat. It broadened to enclose a central row of houses and shops that led past the War Memorial on the Market Hill to the Church. Its bow lay beyond the Church and the church school where we all went, pointing towards the Common with its ditches and 'hills', said to be from Roman times.

Its houses were washed pink and yellow and white, or were in red brick or grey brick, and some had white posts and black chains or small iron railings to enclose minute front gardens. Just a few had exposed black beams. There were huge old chestnut trees in Nethergate Street, yew trees in the churchyard, a wonderful weeping ash like a tent to hide in up the Cemetery, and yet more chestnuts to swing on by the path to the Priory Farm. The castle mound was covered in trees, and trees peeped over the tops of houses from the bottoms of long gardens. Down by the river, on the south side of the castle, were water meadows where cows grazed, and where the slow-moving Stour was partly covered by reeds and water lilies where coots walked on careful feet, and where there were roach and perch and lurking pike. Before the War there was sometimes the sound of a horn and of hounds down by the river: they were otter-hunting. Other huntsmen gathered occasionally on horseback outside the Bell on the Market Hill. Beyond, out into the farmland, fields gently dipped and rose, bordered by thick hedges of hazel, bramble, and white and black thorn, with towering elms. Two small streams, from Chilton and Poslingford to the north, joined together and gently meandered under tall trees and past gardens to join the Stour down by the Station.

On the Market Hill opposite the Town Hall was Grandad's baker's shop: 'F.C. Pashler, Baker and Confectioner.' It stood at the end of a narrow lane which bisected the central row of houses, and connected the Market Hill to the High Street. Neighbours there lived very much cheek-by-jowl, and mostly knew each other's business, but not always. There were some who did keep themselves strictly to themselves.

Growing up in a shop was, I think, a great privilege for me. One became sociable at a very early age. Mother used to pop me with one or two toys into the side window of the shop, where I could play safely on the gently sloping boards inside the low, wire-mesh fence and see and be seen and be part and parcel of the shop life. Also, I was the only child on the Market Hill, and so by the time I was able to ride a tricycle I already knew our neighbours and many others besides, and always found a kindly welcome when I went visiting. By looking up and down the path for my parked tricycle, Mother could usually see where I was.

All our neighbours were old, about as old as Grandad and Gran, and if they had children at home they were as old as Mother, and most were daughters. The first World War had taken many sons, as the War Memorial on the Market Hill showed. Uncle Charles was one of the few living at home, and he had a painful, stiff leg caused by a motor cycle accident in his youth. He was a lonely man, which made him morose at times. He took turns with Uncle Vic to drive the bread van, and helped to make the dough and the loaves and the cakes and pastries, and could ice and decorate a cake like an inspired angel. But I'll come to that later. All the family except Gran and me had dark eyes, almost black, and Uncle Vic in particular had high cheekbones accentuated by his thin frame. He died in his fifties, of Baker's Lung (or so I understand), leaving a family of six children: twin sons, slightly older than me, and four daughters. Aunt Cis, his wife, was stalwart, and kept the family close and true to each other.

At Christmas I was always invited to go to The Party at my cousins', where we were nine with the two girls from next door who were great friends of theirs (and still are, I believe). Bread and butter and paste sandwiches and jelly and cake. It was wonderfully exciting, and we played 'spin the trencher' sitting in a circle. Mother always came to collect me far too soon. I did not have children come back to tea with me, perhaps because we did not have our tea until the shop was shut at six o' clock, and it would have been too much for Gran. In the end I gave up asking. It was just a fact of life. My cousins and I used to play together sometimes on the Castle Bailey, particularly when we could make tents out of old sheets on sticks and string, anchoring the sides with stones. Then we would eat our jam sandwiches at tea time, together with the wasps. But my cousins were like a bunch of grapes, closely-joined and self-sufficient, and most of the time I played with other friends, particularly Dorie.

Home

Our House

Our house was unremarkable, I suppose, painted cream under a grey slate roof, on the south side of the Lane looking across the Market Hill. The door to the Shop was canted at an angle between the window at the front and that in the Lane, and the front door of the house led from Market Hill into a hallway which looked straight through to the yellow stone sink at the end of the passage. To the left of the hallway was the Front Room, and beyond it the Living Room: on the right was the Shop and the staircase. Beyond again was the Little Kitchen on the left and the Big Kitchen on the right. The 'hallway' became the 'passage' where the life of the house began, for the Front Room was hardly ever used. The hall had linoleum and a runner of carpet, two pictures and a hat-and-coat stand: the passage had coconut matting laid over its bricks, a run of hooks for coats and hats used every day, and a photo of Grandad playing the whistle in a band. A door led down to the cellar, which was under the Shop, the Front Room and the Living Room.

The Front Room had an un-used smell for Gran didn't like pulling down the window because of the dust and dirt getting in from the street. It was used at Christmas, and Uncle Charles had made a hole in the wall so that the flex of the wireless could pass through from the Living Room behind, allowing us to set it up and hear the King's speech and other programmes. For the rest of the year, when the wireless was in the Living Room, a cork plugged the hole. There was a carpet in the Front Room, on the usual lino, and a three-piece suite. There was a grandfather clock, too, with a picture of the sun and moon on its face, and a glass-fronted cabinet where Gran kept her best teapot and cups and saucers and milk jug, and a glass bowl, and a few silver-plated things just in case we had company. But we never did, or hardly ever. Just very occasion-ally, once in a blue moon, some relatives from Bury or some other distant place might drop by, and if it was a Sunday as it usually was, then we'd all gather in the Front Room, of course. The conversation rarely flowed: more often it went forward in hops and skips, with lots of stops and starts. 'Do you remember...?' 'Whatever happened to...?' 'Ah...' But perhaps that is just how it seemed to me, for I didn't know any of the people being talked about.

On the wall hung a stern photograph of a

heavily-bearded John Thomas Pashler, Grandad's father, and his equally stern-looking wife, and under their eye I was meant to do my piano practice. But the keys were very stiff and yellow, and practicing was extremely boring. It was much more fun twiddling round on the revolving stool. Mother would look in crossly. The teacher who taught me was the same Miss Stokoe who had taught her, and was strict, but made little progress with me. Mother was a good player, but not even she wandered in there for a tune very often. She needed encouragement and someone to play to, perhaps.

Now the cellar *was* remarkable, as I realized later on, for people from archaeological societies would come and ask to see it. We kept the coal for the furnace and fireplaces down there and it smelt of coal dust and damp, and its floor was simply packed earth. What people came to see was its groined stone roof and central pillar, like those in a church only much shorter. But for us it was just a place we used to the best of our ability and limited imagination. Indeed, I don't think we had any imagination about it. Although it is true that Uncle Charles had tried to find the whereabouts of a rumoured underground passage leading to the Church and Priory, but very little had come of that. Nothing, in fact, but a bit of a dent in the wall...

And so we had a steel-mesh safe on the stairs, where food could be safely protected from heat and mice and occasionally a rat. Great excitement then. Blackie the cat was called for and popped down the steps. A little later, Uncle Charles would go down with his walking stick and a torch.

'Has he got it?' Gran would call anxiously.

'No. The b******s still there,' Uncle would say, as he hopped awkwardly up the steps as quickly as he could. The lethal battle then continued, unseen in the dark, and we were all caught up in the excitement.

'You going down again, Charles?'

'Give it a bit yet.'

Then down he'd go again. 'Well?' called Gran, still anxious. 'Has he got it?'

''*Course* he has!' called Uncle, as though there could never have been the least possible fraction of doubt in *his* mind, ever. The three of them came up, Blackie to pats and praises and a nice saucer of milk, and the very dead rat carried by its tail to the dustbin. Blackie was a good ratter and mouser, and spent most of the day recovering in the dusty, sunny window of the flour loft.

In the War, Mother, and Bessie and Emma the 'helps' gave the cellar a good sweeping and brushing and it became our air raid shelter. Anyone who wanted could come and bring their camp beds. The Hurry's had their own cellar at the butcher's next door, but sometimes the Thompsons from the Garage came, and others whom Grandad had met at the Swan that evening would look in for an hour or so, or else kip down with the rest of us, depending on what was happening outside. Our presence must have given what mice and rats there were a bit of a shock: or else Blackie had been put down to make a clearance beforehand.

The Living Room

But to get back upstairs. None of the rooms we lived in could have been much more than ten feet wide, if that, and certainly no longer. Yet in the Living Room (whose door had a window with a lace curtain, so that Gran could see who had come into the shop when the bell rang) we had a fireplace and two armchairs, a couch under the window, with its head to the Front Room and its foot to Gran's chair by the fire, a narrow table whose wide leaves came up to seat six of us round three sides of it at mealtimes, and a wireless with plenty of wires, sitting on a high shelf on brackets over the head of the couch.

I say 'high'. Nothing was high. Fortunately none of us was tall. Apart from the small chairs and my stool to sit on at mealtimes, in winter there was always Gip the black-

and-tan mongrel in front of the fire, the cat sometimes on Gran's chair, and a singing brown enamel kettle on the trivet. A toasting fork always hung at the side, and on the mantelpiece stood a black clock, and above it a mirror just too high to see into. Grandad's chair stood in the corner on the other side of the fireplace against cupboards, one of which was tall and opened rarely, for it meant moving his chair to get into it. There we knitted and embroidered and read and listened to 'Monday night at Eight', and 'In Town Tonight' and, of course, Uncle Mac and David on 'Children's Hour', and I made scrap books if I was very careful, and Gran and Mother did mending.

During the week Grandad usually went off somewhere at the end of the morning, if there was time before dinner. Sometimes even if there was not, I seem to remember. He'd get his collar and stud from the corner cupboard in the Little Kitchen, and then his tie, put them on and off he'd go. If not to the Swan, then to the Bell, where he also had a corner chair in the snug that was 'his'. Only very rarely did he go to the Bear. In the Swan and the Bell he might meet up with a stranger, perhaps a commercial traveller passing through, who knows, but someone new on the horizon to talk with, someone fresh from outside, and that he did so love.

If it had been really enjoyable, then when I

sat on his lap in the armchair after dinner, he would doze off and be no company at all. He usually dozed off anyway, but before that we could chat while I played with his watch chain or showed him how quickly I could knit now. (That he would know by the way my arms moved, and all the rest of me, because it was important he understood). But he always dozed off. I liked to comb his hair and make new partings, and he quite enjoyed it except when he said my knees dug into him. But when the inevitable happened I would slip quietly down and leave him to discover his new hairstyle for himself when he woke up. Which didn't always happen immediately...

When I sat on his lap, he had a special Grandad smell. A little bit like his desk on the counter, a little bit like the food we ate, and a little bit that was just him and no-one else.

He used some funny words – 'sub rosa' for instance, which apparently meant 'to keep things secret'. You also had to be 'on the qui vive' at times, which meant that you had to keep a sharp look out for goodness only knew what, and that brought a bit of excitement with it. 'Perspicacious' was one of his very favourite words, and when things were finished and as they should be, then they were ' all Sir Garney'.

He loved to read. Most of Dickens, and in

particular the Pickwick Papers, were what he preferred. But he liked the Trials of Christmas Humphreys too, and it was he that led me to Rider Haggard to enjoy what he called 'a good yarn'. Then Mr Andrews who lived near the Bell lent him bound copies of the Strand Magazine, and these gave him particular pleasure. Uncle Charles and I liked them too, and they kept us going for a long time. The grown-ups used Mrs Wiffen's lending library, where the men could have good old stalwarts like Sherlock Holmes and Edgar Wallace, and where Gran and Mother could find their romances.

Our Bedroom, Tonsils and Angels

For quite a long time, until I was about eight or even older, I slept with Mother in the big bed in her room over the Shop. Like all the beds we knew, it was made of iron and had a feather mattress, a bolster and valances, and its eiderdown cover had flowers on a black background. When it was cold, there was always a lovely warm gurgling hot water bottle in a knitted cover to cuddle. I knew that room inside out and upside down, having spent so much time there with earache when younger. There were forty eight large butterflies going round the frieze at the top of the wallpaper, and the narrow stripes going down also had butterflies between them, really good ones, almost natural-looking, some brown, some blue, most of them sort of familiar, but smaller than those on the frieze.

The door was varnished black, like all the others and some of the floorboards. The wardrobe faced the foot of the bed, its double doors curtained in orange cotton. Mother's dressing table stood to one side in the corner by the window, and a mahogany chest of drawers stood on the other side of the window, beside the bed. There was yet another chest between the door and the washstand against the opposite wall. The floor was covered with linoleum and three mats framed the bed.

Because of the earache, I seemed to spend hours and hours there, with colouring crayons and books and little celluloid dolls who also sailed on the water butts in matchboxes. Knees made mountains for them, and the tassels on my dressing gown cord could also be explorers or graceful dancers; and the cracks on the ceiling never failed to produce strange pictures that took one into other landscapes, other worlds. Finally, one could always call for a drink, and hope for some company for a few minutes.

At night, and during the day too, Mother would take a teaspoon filled with olive oil and heat it gently over the candle flame. In it she would soak a small piece of cotton wool and put it in my ear. The warmth was soothing. I would lie there squinting, trying to catch the candle beam between my fingers, listening to the voices coming up the stairs from below. Olive oil for me, in those days, was synonymous with cotton wool and earache. It wasn't until many years later that I learned that you could eat it too.

At last it was decided to have my tonsils out. At home, in the bedroom. A table was somehow brought up the stairs, and I remember lying on it, with Mother standing beside me. Something white was put against my face and rainbows appeared. The next thing I knew was that I was in Uncle Charles' bed, and only allowed something called junket, which was slippery and really terrible. It was true that my throat was sore, but because it had all been done in familiar surroundings it wasn't really frightening.

Sometimes, early in the morning, something would bang against the shop door and there would be a soft, multitudinous noise outside. Lifting the lace half-curtain you'd see the whole place full of a creamy surge of bothered black-faced sheep, the silly ones getting wedged behind the telephone kiosk opposite or getting stuck in doorways. After- wards, Gran took a stiff broom and swept any stray pellets from the doorstep. But, for some reason, they stopped driving them through Clare after the war started.

From the bedroom, too, we hung the Union Jack, its pole jammed fast by the sash window, for the yearly Flower Shows, and King George the Fifth's and Queen Mary's Jubilee, and the Coronation. We attached red, white and blue paper chains and bells wherever we could reach. They were all stored up in the attic with the apples, and looked a bit more part-worn each time they appeared, and just very slightly haphazard. Some people's were absolute wonders, though, and made us all feel very proud of Clare.

In that room, too, early in the morning when Mother had gone downstairs and I had turned the bedclothes head to foot and mentally furnished the room on the ceiling, where it looked much nicer, Grandad sometimes came in with a small, slim bar of chocolate wrapped in red paper. Then he would tell me about Teddy and their conversation earlier on, for Teddy always spent the night fast asleep in his pram under the glass window case in the Shop. And Mother would be so *cross* with him over the chocolate. Poor Mother. She was right, of course, but how lovely it was.

On Sunday morning, when Gran had gone down with Mother to get the breakfast ready, I would clamber into Gran and Grandad's bed to be read to. The Water

Babies I quite liked, but preferred to hear about the school at Acorn Corner, kept by a Gnome who had a lot of trouble with a very naughty washerwoman who *would* use too much starch. While he read, he let me use Mother's tweezers to pull out the hairs that grew on his nose. 'Steady on there,' he'd say occasionally, but he was very patient.

Sometimes, Grandad would go to bed early. He came quite slowly up the stairs, and would pause to say 'night, night' softly, in case I was asleep, but sometimes I was still quite wide awake. Waiting, I would hear his and Gran's bed creak as he got into it, and then I would creep slowly and silently to their room and say 'Can I come in your bed?' And if he wasn't too tired I was allowed to get in Gran's side, and then ask him to sing songs to me. They had to follow a certain pattern, and in this way neither of us forgot any (or almost not). He sang in a whisper: Daisy, Daisy... She was a sweet little dicky-bird... After the Ball was Over... The Grandfather Clock... Daddy wouldn't buy me a Bow-Wow... Where did you get that Hat?... I knocked 'em in the Old Kent Road... Two little girls in blue... My old Man... At Trinity Church I met my doom ... and countless others: about 45 in all. I used to count them on my fingers, and sometimes we had to rack our brains for the missing ones, but that made it all the more fun. He knew so many. On light evenings, watching the fruit trees opposite go blacker and blacker in the twilight, we would play I Spy, or try and guess whose step it was going past, or round the back of the Bear. We always knew old Billy Yabham's stumbling unevenness by the sound of his big boots and blakeys. Then we would both be suddenly quiet. 'Quick,' he'd say, 'off you go, they're coming.' Poor Gran, with her hair done up in her Lady Jayne curlers, could be so cross if she found me not tucked up fast asleep in the other room.

There, too, I was convinced I saw an angel, and probably my guardian one, I thought. When I told Miss Wiffen at Sunday School – for she was talking about angels, and it seemed appropriate to mention it – she didn't move a muscle under her severe brimmed hat, just looked at me. What was it like? she asked. I said it was a light over the washstand, and so it had been. A very small, bright light, which became a bigger glow, just quickly, and then had gone again. It didn't sound much when talked about, but I was quite sure a sort of curtain had slipped, and that I'd seen something that was always there, but not to be seen. Anyway, *I* knew even if she couldn't. Nowadays, of course, I'm not so sure, which is a little sad.

It was there in that room when caught unawares by German bombers or Doodlebugs, that we would scrabble out of the sheets and get under the bed, Mother pushing the chamber pot to a safe distance. How cold that lino could be! But that only happened when we'd trusted to luck, wanting to be comfy rather than spend the night in the cellar.

At that time Chrissie would sometimes arrive on her upright bicycle. She was a friend of Gran's, and would stay the night in the small fourth bedroom at the back. She always brought a jar of honey with her, and lovely honey it was too. Chrissie was also called Cry, which I thought meant that she had a great sorrow too terrible to be told and that she cried a lot. I never got to know her, or anything more about her, but later on I had that bedroom all to myself, and I remember still the pure pleasure of having my own place, with my own things in it, and rearranging those few things again and again until it was right. In the drawer of the dressing table were coins from India and old photographs. No one knew who they were of, but they were treasures of course, full of romance.

The Little Kitchen, and Emma

In summer, meals were taken at the scrubbed table in the Little Kitchen. This was where Emma did the washing every Monday. Behind the door from the passage, and backing on to the Living Room, was the mangle; then the unused fireplace, and next to that, in a recess under its own small window, was the copper. Behind the table was yet another door leading into the cobbled yard, but this was only used on Mondays when Emma hung the washing on the line.

She was a powerfully built woman, with large bones, and did the washing and some ironing and scrubbing for Gran. I used to watch her take the sheets from the copper, let them cool a little, and then wring them with her strong wrists. After that, she folded them and laid them in the zinc bath, ready to go through the mangle. One by one she would push the folded sheet ends between the pale wooden rollers and turn the big handle to squeeze them through, the water running back into the bath as it was pressed out. The sheets zig-zagged slowly, in gentle, even, folds into the linen basket at the back of the mangle, dry enough to be hung out. When they were ready to come in again, two people were needed to pull them straight and fold them, ready for ironing. After which they were put on the clotheshorse to air in the sun, or by the fire, or in the bakehouse overnight.

I remember how she liked to sing the same song over and over as she scrubbed the floors in the shop and passage and kitchens and bakehouse. It was a song from the beginning of the War. Having her head down made her nose run, so every few words were punctuated by a sniff.

'You are my sunshine' – sniff – 'my only sunshine' – sniff – and so on to the end. Then she would begin again.

When I was much smaller I had wanted to do the same as Emma, and scrub the step from the yard to the Little Kitchen myself. So many times I had watched her, with her pail and scrubbing brush and grey cloth made of thick string. I knew exactly how to do it. You SLOPPED the wet cloth all over the stone, then you dipped the brush – just so – into the pail to wet it, and rubbed it with the soap. With the soapy brush you made big circles all over the stone, and that made patterns of white bubbles; when that was properly done you took the cloth again and splooshed it around in the pail. Then you gathered it up and wrung it twice, three times, and FLUNG it onto the step. Having wiped the step very carefully, you then rinsed the cloth and wrung it out again. This time, as you wiped the step, you went into the corners, getting it all nice. Then it was done. For a treat I was allowed to do it when Emma wasn't there, and sometimes did the Betts' back step as well, for one step seemed too little for all the equipment. Gran would have folded a rubber apron and tied it round me as high up under my arms as she could to stop me becoming drenched, and didn't really want me to do it at all because she had so many other things to think of and didn't have time to keep an eye on me. Mother would have been in the bakehouse or the Shop, also too busy to attend to all of this performance.

I haven't mentioned Bessie, but she was always there. She was Gran's daily help, came before breakfast and stayed until tea-time. She came every day except Sundays, a quiet girl, rather solemn, but I never heard Gran complain about her so they must have got on well together. So Bessie was the one who made six at mealtimes, if we were all there. On Mondays there could be seven for dinner (for Emma ate with us then), unless Uncle Charles was out for most of the day on a bread round. There would be a great scraping of chairs on the brick floor as we settled round the table in the Little Kitchen, and on fine days the sun poured in through the larger window that looked onto the yard.

I loved moving up into the Little Kitchen for it was so light and airy after the living room. Peggles and primroses and violets stood in big and small jam jars whose water shone like silver on the windowsill, and you could smell them while you ate. Dorie was allowed to keep tadpoles and sticklebacks on their copper, but mine had to go outside where Blackie sat or lay unmoving a short way away, intent, watching everything minutely. I hope to goodness, now, that the poor fish were not traumatized.

Running back from the window with the peggles was a shelf, ending at a corner cupboard. In here we kept iodine, witch hazel, Vaseline, TCP and bandages, all used at one time or another for grazes and bloody knees, stings or cuts. Vick Vapour Rub also lived there, with Wintergreen Ointment and a bottle of Eucalyptus. But it also housed Grandad's cutthroat razor and shaving soap and brush, his hairbrush and comb, and a small standing mirror. Next to the cupboard hung his strop. Here he liked to shave.

First he would fetch a basin of hot water from the kettle that was always singing on the oil stove in the Big Kitchen opposite, or from the tap by the oven in the bakehouse, and then, taking the razor, he'd pull out the long blade from its yellow bone handle and strop it on the leather strap. Up and down, up and down, quickly, neatly. When that was done he would make himself a thick, soapy beard, lathering round and round on the grey stubble and down under his chin. (It might well be after 8.30 or even 9 by now, between two batches of bread-making, for he was up at five o'clock every morning). Peering closely into the mirror he'd move his chin to stretch the skin and make a smooth swathe down one cheek, and so on, dipping the blade into the basin every now and then to clean it, leaving little bobbly mounds of white froth; round under the nose, this way, that way; and finally, with his other hand upside down to pull his cheek up, he'd go down the sides of his neck.

'You've missed a bit!'

'Where?'

'Just there!'

Then 'How's that?'

Uncle Charles shaved at the stone sink.

The Yard

The yard, which we shared with the Betts next door, was cobbled. It contained our water-butt, a clothes line, and a few pockets of earth at the foot of the wall dividing us from the Parkers, where patches of frothy pink London Pride grew quite freely.

On Mondays, Emma hung the washing on the line in the yard, and in late summer and early autumn Gran would lay out the green walnuts on tin trays, balanced carefully on chairs to dry in the sun and so prepare them for pickling.

The water butt was one of Dorie's and my chief centres of play where, standing on wooden crates, we sailed our small celluloid dolls in matchboxes round the world, to unnamed islands, and through tempests that upset their boats – but being celluloid they never drowned, of course, and recovered in no time at all. They sailed unaware of the creatures around and below which we called pollywiggles – mosquito larvae, as I discovered many years later. Dorie had an oblong and lower water butt by her back door, and there our dolls had similar adventures.

The yard also had the Betts' outside WC at the end of their kitchen, against the wall; and further along the wall, next to our water butt and opposite the end of Grandad's oven, was their wash house. Beyond that was our WC. Its seat was long, bare scrubbed wood, the chain strong and business-like, and the walls washed bright Dolly-blue. On frosty nights it had a small oil lamp to keep the cistern from freezing up.

If one didn't quite close the door it was possible to sit and watch Mr Lee and Arthur Deeks tailoring away in their upstairs work room along the Lane, making the good, sensible clothes needed by country people, because their window overlooked our lav. Although I'm sure they never looked at me because they were both very Baptist – well, Mr Lee was, anyway. You could see the sunlight glinting on Arthur's round spectacles and his bald head, and he always had a tape measure round his neck. And in the late spring high branches of lilac from their garden hung over the wall, right by the door.

The Shop

The Shop had its double door obliquely under the jutting-out corner of Mother's and my bedroom. A bell hung on one side, so that we could hear when anyone came in. The floor was of plain boards. Two big windows each had a sloping wooden display shelf, the one to the lane surrounded by the crinkly wire-mesh 'fence', and the main one on the street encased in glass with lift-up panels on either side. I can well remember reaching in for cakes that customers wanted, holding up the glass side with one hand and bending into the case and reaching with the other. Grandad always kept glass wasp-catchers with beer in them nearby, for the wasps dearly loved the sticky Eccles cakes and jam puffs. We had sticky fly-catchers too, that curled down in twirls from the ceiling and got blacker and blacker until they needed changing.

The Counter stood solidly in the middle, with Grandad's sloping desk at one end against the glass case. Once you opened the lid, out came a powerful smell of tobacco from the tin and leather pouch he kept there, replenished every so often when I was sent on an errand to Mr Deeks the tobacconist at the top of Station Road. 'An ounce' – or was it two? – or four? – 'of St Julien tobacco please.' Mr Deeks, quite often in shirt-sleeves and braces, with shiny elastic arm-bands like Grandad wore, but very neat and clean, had a large, pale face and moved slowly. He would turn and slip carefully off his stool to fetch and weigh the tobacco (which looked exactly like a sweet, probably dyed coconut, that Susie Stiff sold), tuck it neatly into Grandad's pouch, and that would be that. Then it wouldn't be long before Grandad was tucking it into his pipe after dinner or tea, sucking and drawing on it with his cheeks in, using this match, then another, and perhaps even another after that. Mr Deeks had a housekeeper who was very short – probably from some growth defect, but she didn't seem to mind and nor did anybody else. She was a bright, brisk little body and regularly went to and fro on sturdy legs to Mrs Wiffen's tiny library on the Bell corner with arms full of books.

The only other things in Grandad's desk were pen-holders with nibs, a rubber, old bottles of ink, some pencils, scraps of paper and bill-headings – and all smelt of tobacco, especially the rubber. On the sloping top was the Order Book, and by its side hung a pencil on a string. The counter had two slits in it, one for silver and the near one for copper, and a drawer underneath for the giving of change. A large loaf after the War cost five pennies (old ones, of course), and a small one exactly half that – tuppence halfpenny. Before the War they cost even less, but I don't remember how much. As there were 240 pennies in the pound then, it might seem that bread was cheap – but a farm labourer might earn no more than ten shillings – half a pound – a week and not every family could pay its bread bills. Grandad would readily settle for a rabbit or something else easier to come by than cash. The 'thirties were hard years. Uncle Bertie once found an old man sitting in a pub in Saffron Walden with his head on his arms. 'Ah, Master,' he said 'oi've bin a-woisenin'. Toimes is bad. Money's got in tew big 'eaps, an' tew few...'

Behind the counter were shelves with more drawers underneath. On top of the drawers there would sometimes be warm sponge cakes cooling, some as special orders with golden crusted sugar tops and light as a feather. There was a pair of scales for weighing slabs of butter, or ounces of the shiny, brightly-coloured sweets and wrapped toffees from jars on the shelves, and their little round weights made a high pyramid of brass just behind.

One summer, Mother, who loved to cook as well, was excited and happy for a sort of refrigerator had arrived and stood proudly next to the scales. She began making ice-cream to sell, but I think it was a fairly short-lived enterprise though the ice-cream tasted quite nice if a bit custardy. She also had competition for the ice-cream man used to come round on his tricycle, ringing his bell loudly to let everyone know he had arrived; and he had more variety, I suppose.

If you stood as a customer with the Lane to your back and the Market Hill window to your left, you could turn to the right and look into The Recess. This housed Over-flows. Its entrance was up a step through a double metal arch – which must have been the support for the wall between Uncle Charles' and our bedrooms. The Recess contained a lot. There were big tins of this and that and a glass-fronted cupboard with more of Gran's prized and barely-used best china. Her stone jars of dandelion, rhubarb and parsnip wine stood in a row under my toy shelves on the left and just occasionally one burst with a tremendous to-do. In the middle was a muddle of boxes – tea chests holding goodness-knows what, or perhaps kept there, empty, in case they might 'come in' one day. The shelves to the right were dark, and housed things to do with the business – glacé cherries, currants, sultanas, catalogues of beautiful sugar flowers, home-made jams, un-understood things. Once or twice – to my great shame now – we hid a captured newt or two in a shallow glass bowl, smuggled in when Gran wasn't looking. Of course they always disappeared, poor things. Where to is beyond my imagining, or wish to know.

On the tea chests I remember assembling my first block puzzles of sheep and lambs and cows. The shelves behind me slowly filled up with other things such as favourite books, piles of comics, a doll's house – well, more a suburban villa with even a Mr and Mrs installed, a tin oven with saucepans that I had so coveted and almost immediately neglected and a beautifully-dressed, jointed, French doll (a present from Auntie Hilda Betts next door). But, somehow, I never felt really connected to these three things, and eventually I gave them to an insistent Gypsy, for they often came into the Shop looking at things and selling wooden clothes pegs or sprigs of white heather from a big basket on their arms. I only felt guilty about the doll, not wanting to hurt Auntie Hilda, but the Gypsy had said how much her little girl would love it, and I really didn't at all. But Teddy and Dinah belonged utterly.

Teddy had always been there. I don't remember his arrival, and his departure is not yet (he is in a box in the airing cupboard with other precious things, loved by others). Dinah was the doll nearest my heart because she was the right size, tightly huggable because she was stuffed, and had the nicest nature, being amiable and uncritical. Although her body was stuffed, she had a china face, eyes that closed and black hair. Her yellow dress with two frills was stitched onto her. So she always looked the same, and *was* the same Dinah, whatever else I put her into. She remained placid though possibly uncomfortable, and she and Teddy were, without doubt, good friends. But Dinah departed long, long ago, and strangely, I don't remember her going. Teddy and she were my real other personae, my real communicados-without-words. They absorbed like Labrador dogs, and gave the same affection and loyalty, in total silence, with total understanding. Though one of them could talk back sometimes, it seemed.

It was Grandad who found out that Teddy could talk. That didn't surprise me. Teddy would, of course, talk to a man, and one up so early, when he himself was just waking up in the pram under the glass case. They would talk together while Grandad had a glass of beer from the short barrel under the scales, after seeing to the furnace and the first batch of bread.

From the Shop we could see all that happened and all who passed without barely stirring an inch. Only at night and on Sundays were the faded dark blue-green blinds rolled down – and for funerals, when Gran and Mother might lift them just a little from the edge to see what was passing. Sometimes even the upstairs and front room blinds were lowered as well. It all depended on who it was. Then they were pulled up again, and the shop continued its business.

When it was hot a blind was let down over the pavement, where the grating lay over the old steps leading down to the cellar. That was where the sacks of coal were humped down. Because of the sun and heat on the front door's paint, Gran also wedged it open and hung up a striped canvas curtain, and that gave a little welcome draught up the passage. But the bakehouse itself was like an oven then, and wasps were everywhere.

Throughout the day the Shop bell rang. Not every minute or every five minutes, but steadily so that if you settled to do something you could be sure it wouldn't be long before ... there it would go again. Everyone had his or her bread wrapped in tissue paper from the top of the pile on the end of the counter, and it was rare not to pass the time of day. One thing would lead to another; sometimes just a passing remark on the weather, or a kindly word; sometimes an old grievance had an airing, or perhaps there would be a scent of gossip, or even gossip itself. Even as quite a small child, when I first learned to serve customers, I was told to say always 'Good Morning' or 'Good afternoon' to each person who came in, and that was also how everyone greeted each other in the street. Well, no not quite. Hats were half-lifted also, and old men had a conspiratorial sideways shake of the head. And some old folk, and even some younger ones, if they spoke really broad Suffolk, would address each other either as 'boh' for a man or 'moh' for a woman. Occasionally, too, you'd hear cows referred to as 'coos' and houses as 'housen'.

In winter, a round Valor stove was lit to give a little warmth in the Shop, and when the afternoons pulled in quickly the gas light over the counter was lit too. Only the Shop, the Front Room and the Living Room had gas lights: the kitchens and bedrooms, and even the bakehouse, had to have oil lamps or candles. A small lamp always burned in winter over the yellow stone sink, and sent a faint, soft glow down the passage. Another one burned in the Big Kitchen, by the window to the Lane. It was a hushed, gentle, warm light: it was always a special time of year for me when we began lighting them. Although, of course, it would have been difficult to manage so well without the gas lights, for they allowed us to read, and embroider and knit, but we still sometimes used a big oil lamp instead – especially if we had forgotten to get a new mantle.

A gas mantle was the most wonderful, delicate, biscuity tube of net which, from pure white, turned sooty black when used. It hung from a metal piece screwed into the ceiling connection, and had to be put in place with the greatest care. Two little chains hung down at the two ends of a cross-bar, and pulling one produced the flow of gas to be lit. This was done with a match held very gently near the mantle. It then took hold and began to glow. When it began to roar, the flow was adjusted, and then a softish, white-yellow light came over everything. To turn it off you simply pulled the higher chain. Glass shades, bell-shaped and fluted, covered the mantle in all three rooms. Changing the mantle was quite a performance, to be done with patience, usually by the women.

The Loft, Making the Dough and the Loaves, and Christmas Morning...

From the Big Kitchen was another staircase leading to the flour loft above. If he wasn't rushed, Grandad would piggyback me up to the maize bin at the top of the stairs, sit me on the lid to take off my shoes, and then open it and plant me inside. Like that I could not get out, was quite safe, and could see all that went on as I trampled the nubbly corn. It smelt quite different up there. The

49

maize smelt, the flour smelt, it was dusty, and more often than not old Blackie would be sleeping off the night before on the warm windowsill overlooking the yard. He never stirred as Grandad weighed great sacks of flour on the big flat weighing machine, and then manoeuvred them to a trap door to empty them into the dough machine below. Sometimes he weighed me too, and then we'd go down again.

The dough machine stood in a corner of the bakehouse at the far end of the trough, away from the furnace. It was a big, round metal drum painted green with wording embossed on it, standing on four spread legs and with a large wheel to one side. Attached to the wheel was a handle which had to be turned and turned, round and round, now by Uncle Charles, then by Uncle Vic, and then by Grandad, first with one hand, then the other, and as the dough slowly stiffened, with both. It was very heavy work, especially if there were only two of them. Finally the drum was stopped and opened and the dough dropped heavily and cleanly into the long wooden trough to rise.

Once risen, great wedges were cut from it, hung over arms and heaved onto the Side – a long, well-scrubbed bench – opposite. Quite often two of them worked in unison, side by side, slicing off pieces of about the right size, throwing them onto the scales in front of them, and then adjusting the weight by adding another piece or chopping a piece off. Flour was then scattered by hand, just enough, and then, with arms straight in front of them, they kneaded the dough, a piece in each hand. Flour was sprinkled yet again on the boards and the moulding went on, smooth shapes appearing under their rhythmic hands.

Some were put into greased and floured oblong tins, large and small: others were left round, and given a cross on top; or were made long and sliced four or five times slantwise. Smaller rounds were slapped on top of larger ones, and then the sharp knife and four quick turns made sure that each cottage loaf had regular cuts from top to bottom. The twists were the most fun to watch being made: three fat sausage shapes with tapering ends were plaited together and the result was a lovely pattern that began from nothing, swelled out, and then returned to nothing again. All the loaves were brushed with something or other, and then Grandad slid his peel – a kind of flat, long-handled wooden shovel – under them and placed them just where he wanted them in the brick oven.

After that, a keen eye had to be kept on the furnace and the need to move loaves around in the oven. The life of the Bakery hung on the heat of the oven, when it was just right, and again when the loaves were properly done. Or when the pastries were ready to come out, and the cakes cooked. Then the peels were brought down from the bakehouse ceiling, the heat from the oven flooded out, and fast and furiously the loaves in their tins were removed. 'Whissht!' Grandad would call out, swinging a peel with a scorching tin or loaf on the end to cast it in a flash onto the Side where it slid into the corner or came to a stop against the others. Two batches were baked each day, apart from the cakes and the pastries. In the holidays I was allowed a small patch of bench just inside the door to roll my own piece of dough, depending on the mood of the moment of course and the tensions in the air. But my small, grey offerings never quite matched the others.

And the cakes! Triangular jam puffs; cream horns; jam tarts with shiny crimson centres; maids of honour, their crisp centres smelling of almond; madeleines all dainty in their white coconut flakes, topped with glace cherries; doughnuts, fat and round and dusted with sugar; currant buns; iced Genoese squares; macaroons. At Easter there were Hot Cross Buns, warm and soft and shiny, as brown as freshly-shelled chestnuts, filling your nose and lungs with their spiced fragrance – the whole house even. But this only for a day or so, once a year, for everything had its season, its time, its meaning.

'Mind your backs!' was the cry up and down the passage, when the big wooden trays full of small cakes were brought down to go in the windows. And again when the big cakes were brought down. And the loaves. It was a fraught and furious time. And then the bread had to be stacked on the bench in the cross-passage near the door to the lane, so that the bread orders (Cobergs, Tins, Twists and Cottages) could be handed into the van. Mother helped Gran in the shop, but her main job was to help in the bakehouse. Not the heavy dough work: the men did that, but she did much of the cake mixing.

Bread and cakes were not the only things cooked in the bakehouse for customers. There could be up to fifteen turkeys and geese and large plump chickens to be roasted on Christmas morning, all to be done to their owner's timing, and basted, and moved around. And all, I might say, smelling like food for the gods. The herbs of the different stuffings took over and pervaded every bit of lath and plaster, and every brick was blessed with the scent of succulent juices. A rubicund and hot Grandad did his level best, and excelled, and swelled with pride and glowed with something else. Such hard work it was, but who could blame him for so savouring the satisfaction and pleasure of the people who came to collect their crisp, brown juicy birds?

The Bakehouse: Saturdays and Sundays

Emma scrubbed the bakehouse on Saturday afternoons. She scrubbed the Sides where the dough was moulded, and the lid of the trough, and she scrubbed the brick floor. By late afternoon gone was the sound of the stiff brush and the scrape of the pail being moved, and a quietness and feeling of warm peace began slowly to emerge. The wooden peels lay at rest in the ceiling hooks, and silverfish ran over the white-washed brick wall by the oven. Two or three hams or sides of bacon for customers hung swathed in muslin from the highest point of the bakehouse, which at that point reached up two storeys. From late Autumn to Spring Mother and Gran stood a big oil lamp on the Side, and perhaps a small one on the trough, to give enough light to bath by, and in the warmth of the dying furnace there was still the lingering smell of yeast.

Saturday evening was bath-time, and the men had theirs first leaving them free to go out for the rest of the evening. Down from its nail outside came the zinc bath, and saucepans of hot water from the boiler were poured into it: once the boiler was empty, the saucepans were filled at the passage sink and put on all available oil stoves. Winter was the best time to enjoy the lamplight, and the sight of the heap of black coal just gleaming in the shadow, the feel of the towel warmed on the clothes-horse by the furnace, and then clean, warm winceyette pyjamas.

When I was out and dried and dressed for bed, then Grandad was called for. For I danced for him on Saturday evenings in my clean pyjamas (but also to watch my own shadow come and go on the wall where the silverfish were). He brought his pipe and patiently sat where he was told to, and kept a straight face throughout while Mother cleared away. For me it was a serious time, and Mother found my solemnity and concentration a strange contrast to my contortions and twirlings and ploppings. But Grandad never laughed. Having his pipe in his mouth probably helped.

Sunday dinner was cooked in the Bakehouse on the lid of the dough-trough in the oven of the double-burner Valor oil-stove brought in from the Big Kitchen. There was always a roast with potatoes – sometimes chicken and belly pork, sizzling and crisping together in the same tin. Greens or beans were boiled on top of another oil stove. Yorkshire pudding was eaten with gravy first, or else with Golden Syrup afterwards. Or else there was a fruit pie and custard ... or stewed fruit and custard...

I remember we usually had to wait for Grandad to come home from the Swan or the Bell, and he was always late, and poor Gran got cross and hot and bothered. If he was saucy and unsteady when he came, she flew at him, like the time he called her his 'little yellowhammer' because she was wearing a bright yellow cardigan. If he was morose, we all suffered. Only with me was he always the same, and I loved him unconditionally.

After dinner he fell asleep in his armchair while the table was cleared, the leaves let down, and Gran and Mother went to the kettle that had been put on the oil stove in the Big Kitchen for the washing up. After his snooze it was Gran's turn to fall asleep in her chair, and thereafter the only sound was the turning of the Sunday newspapers until teatime. Mother might do her embroidery, or else we might both go up to the bakehouse and do some knotted-wool rug-making.

Sometimes I went to Sunday School, if there was time after dinner. As we sat and listened to Miss Wiffen telling us stories from the Old Testament, usually in Church and just very occasionally in one of the school rooms, I suppose that each of us saw them happening before our eyes in places that we knew. For instance, Jacob's ladder went up to Heaven from the Bailey Gap where we used to munch our jam sandwiches in the bushes, Solomon lived in the plantation behind a white fence just past the gates of the Priory on Ashen Road, and the Queen of Sheba came slowly and very grandly down the hill from Ovington to join him. David and Goliath fought to the death just outside the Priory gates where it flooded, using the chalky stones you could find in the banks. Old, blind, Isaac sat under one of the trees further up the plantation, while poor Joseph, in his colourful striped robe, was put in the pit just round the corner of the Ashen Road on the way to Mr Bruce's house. He and his brothers had arrived on their camels all the way from Belchamp St Paul's. Noah made his Ark from the big pine tree at the bottom of the Cemetery, and the Tower of Babel was somehow also there.

Samuel had no option but to be in a frame above the piano where Miss Stokoe taught and admonished me roundly. He always looked so safe up there, on his knees, praying in a beam of sunlight, unaffected by nearly an hour of Miss Stokoe's asperity. Ruth, of course, was in the same field as Millet's Gleaners in our bedroom. But for a lot of the time we were so preoccupied with making lilies and rabbits surreptitiously with our clean folded handkerchiefs – particularly if we were in the second pew rather than the front one – that quite a lot escaped our attention. And later on, I'm ashamed to say, for much the same reason, only native wit got us through the Catechism as we delved with our eyes into the woven rush seats of the chairs in the side aisles, trying to remember what we ought to have known.

Sometimes two or three others might come back with me from Sunday School, to pass the rest of the afternoon. We let ourselves in by the door in the Lane, hoping that the bake-house was empty, for under one of the Sides were the big shiny mixing bowls with rounded bottoms just right for sitting in and twiddling round on. To get a start you had to balance on finger tips and push off with one foot, and then with any luck you had a good twiddle before collapsing. Of course it could make you feel dizzy and even unwell after a time, but usually well before that point someone would appear in the doorway, furiously angry with us and with the awful noise we had made on the brick floor. And it couldn't have done the bowls much good either. It was difficult finding quiet games with others you didn't normally play with, but depending on who they were, Dressing-Up could be a good substitute. But as that consisted of draping ourselves elaborately in old lace curtains, caught together with a hair clip or two, as either queens or brides, it wasn't everyone's cup of tea. Sometimes even then they were sent home because we were noisy. So then I read.

Not that there was a lot of choice in the house if I wanted something new. A good hunt had only produced copies of 'Swiss Family Robinson' and 'Westward Ho!', given to Uncle Charles when he was a boy. And they had only one picture, at the front. Learning to enjoy reading books without pictures did not come easily. It was like having a cup of coffee without a cigarette when I was older, and in any case I was not gripped by either of those two books. It was about this time that our Brown Owl, Miss Dean, came to the rescue, and she lent us books from the shelves in her summer-house.

And so the week ends passed, and it was time for the furnace to be lit again early on Monday morning. Then it was all go again, and the oven dictated the timing; all go to get the batches done and out on the rounds in the van; much shouting 'mind your backs' down the passage – and all of this when Gran and Grandad were in their mid to late sixties.

Uncle Charles

It was Grandad who taught me to dance the Polka. In the Bakehouse. Bending down, he took my hands, lifted his left foot high while

I lifted my right one, and off we'd go...

'See me dance the Polka,' we sang,
'See me cover the ground.
See my coat tails flying
As I go round and round...'

And round and round we went. He loved to dance. I've heard it said that when they were young he and Gran were a lovely couple to watch. But Uncle Charles, poor man, was not able to dance, and had a great deal of pain with his leg at times. He used to watch us, nevertheless, with a sort of smile.

He was a lonely person, and not easy to know, and never talked about himself or what he really thought or felt. The nearest I came to him was when occasionally I went on bread rounds with him when I was fourteen or fifteen. Before that, when Dorie and I were younger, he would let the two of us squeeze into the front passenger seat by the long, quivering, gear stick and go for the ride. (And when he wasn't looking or had gone to a house with the bread basket, we would break off enticing pieces of crust to nibble).

In winter, after Sunday dinner, Uncle Charles often went up to the bakehouse and sat on a stool in front of the window, cracking walnuts and dipping them into a neat little pile of salt on the bare boards in front of him, before eating them. Sometimes I'd find a stool and go and join him, and he'd crack nuts for me too, and even allow me a sip of his port, which was lovely and sweet.

Or, perhaps he had a cake to ice for a birthday, or a tiered one for a wedding, or Christmas cake orders. Whatever it was, the performance with its own special ritual never ceased to fascinate me. The cakes would have been marzipanned, and allowed to dry out to just the right point, and now they were placed carefully on their individual silver boards, and then onto the turntable. Egg-whites were whisked just so, and gradually the sieved icing sugar was added until it was glossy, and he knew exactly when it was ready. Taking a palette knife he smoothed some over the top and down the sides, swiftly, deftly, and finished with a small flat scraper to leave no seam anywhere at all. Each cake was treated in the same way.

Then he made the greaseproof paper cone to hold the icing for piping, cut the point off neatly, and dropped down into it the particular metal icing pipe he needed for the next stage. Placing the paper cone with its metal tip into a special upright holder, he would spoon as much icing as he needed into it, fold and tuck the end in, and squeeze it till the icing came out the other end.

Then it began – the smooth, even, rhyth-mical piping, with loops and whorls that always met up perfectly as he worked his way round. Different pipes were used for double scallops, and the stars, and as he worked and turned, and stood back for a moment, with a quick passing suck at the nozzle to tidy it up, he whistled quietly to himself.

There were catalogues of sugar flowers that I loved to look at, in their serried ranks down the pages, on a black background to bring out the colour of each dahlia or narcissus petal. To my great disappointment he rarely used such things, but the photographs were beautiful. Yet no more so than his finished, wonderfully iced cakes. That he was good at, and could be proud of.

He seemed to quite enjoy my company later on – perhaps it was just the fact that it was young female company, and he could point me out as his niece. It was nearly dark sometimes, when we got home, depending on how long it had taken to deliver bread to the Fox and Hounds or the Green Man while I sat and waited in the van.

Then, swinging himself with his stiff leg onto the driving seat, he'd bang the door shut. Everything on the van banged. A sort of tinny noise. The doors on the back banged, my door banged, the whole thing banged and rattled. And shook.

'Well, me Ol' Beauty,' he'd say. 'Off we go again!'

He was happy. That was nice. The van banged into motion, the long gear stick with its round handle shook mightily, and we'd sing the current popular songs, laughing at our mistakes, and barely able to hear our voices which were shaken and wobbled by the old brown van as it rattled and bumped and shook us all the way round the winding roads through the dusk. And so we went, the last loaves rustling and jumping up and down behind us.

Mother would be waiting to count the money from his worn brown leather pouch with the two pockets – one for coppers, the other for silver – and do the accounts. Then, before going to bed, she and Gran would make themselves a hot milky drink. Slippery Elm for Gran, and usually Horlicks for Mother, and then they would take the big oil lamp to the Little Kitchen table, where Gran would take out Grandad's shaving mirror from the corner cupboard and painstakingly do up her hair in Lady Jayne curlers, sipping her drink and having one or two sponge finger biscuits in between times. Then they would be peacefully together, having time for each other. Mother was very close to Gran, very protective.

The Swan...

The Swan on Sundays

There were two entrances to the Swan from the High Street. One, on the corner, led into the Bar where Grandad never went. The other, at the front, was a double door with engraved glass panels, opening onto a red-and-black tiled passage. As you went through those doors, the smell of stale beer was always there, even though old Peter, the half-sharp man who did odd jobs, washed the floors every morning. It had probably got into the wood itself and nothing in a hundred years would budge it now.

On the right of the passage was the Tap Room and that, with its range stove, was really the family living room. It was always warm, of course, but the varnish on the walls and settles made it seem very dark. Straight ahead down the passage was the Bar parlour. Grandad never headed for there either. His spot was in the corner of the Snug by the fire, and the Snug was on the left behind the bar.

The Snug was almost minuscule, with Grandad's chair by the fire in the far corner next to a table where cribbage was played (and that was a game he enjoyed) with perhaps another seven or eight chairs side by side as close as can be. I believe it was a room where only men went.

Sometimes, on Sunday mornings before dinner, it was my job to take the small bottle Gran gave me, and the shilling, and reach up to knock on the hatch window of the Snug in the passage and put the bottle and shilling on the shelf. 'Auntie' Newton took both from me and gave me back the bottle containing a colourless liquid which I took to Gran. As I grew taller my eyes met Grandad's in the corner chair, and he winked. But no word passed. I wasn't meant to let him see me, and never told Gran.

On Sunday evenings in late Spring and Summer, when it was nice, we often took a walk – Gran, Grandad, Mother and I – and sometimes it was just up by the Cemetery, round the Backside Fields and over the stile into the field at the back of the Swan where Harry Newton kept a donkey and some chickens and geese and his pigs. It might be it was time for the evening service in the Congregational Chapel over the fence, and as we passed, picking our way through the nettles, bent on crisps and lemonade (or whatever) we would perhaps hear the last hymn being sung. They really did sing out: not at all like in Church where one's own voice seemed to be so loud one took pains to keep it quiet in case you got the note wrong. We always stopped for a moment to gaze at the white bristly pigs with their pink eyes under pale eyelashes, and see if there were any piglets, for we knew that the fat old sows could quite carelessly lie on them and squash them to death. But surely Old Peter and Mr Newton would keep a good eye on them? 'No need to fear,' said Grandad, moving off.

On those light Sunday evenings it was the Bar parlour we went to, where the late sun poured in from the west and made it seem quite jolly. Not that it really was, for in fact it was rather bare, with an empty fireplace, 'parquet' lino on the floor, upright chairs placed around the walls, and a table on coconut matting in the middle. It had one or two trotting prints and mirrors engraved with advertisements. But there were always other Sunday droppers-in to chat to, people one rarely saw otherwise. And there could be kittens to visit in the barn outside. It might be there was another girl there like me, well-known to Mrs Newton, and we would be allowed to explore upstairs, just quickly and quietly. The stairs opposite the Tap Room were in the ubiquitous dark varnish, with a red-patterned stair carpet and brass rods. The landing sloped, and creaked mightily: the beds had sumptuous eiderdowns which we carefully bounced on; and there was even a bathroom. It was all very nice.

Boxing Night at the Swan

This was *the* night of the year, when Gran would put on scent of violets, take her fox fur and turn out the oil stove in the Big Kitchen; when Mother kept powdering her nose, all nervous and excited; and when I, in a new winter dress and indoor shoes, having had a rest in the afternoon, would take *my* little bag with its clean hankie inside. The hot water bottles were in the beds, the lamp was in the WC, and the house was about to be emptied.

'Ready?' said Grandad. He always was. And off we'd go, out of the door and into the Lane.

'Have you got the torch, Charles?'... Then 'Did I turn off the oil stove?' No one could remember, and back Gran would go to make sure, and we'd wait for her. Of course she had. She always had, but best to make sure.

Everywhere was deserted, and pitch black. In whispers, we would cross over to Lufkins the grocers and Mrs Ince's wool shop next door. Past the accumulator shop and the glass and furniture shop next to it. On we'd go, like happy moles, waiting to hear the voices coming through the Swan's windows, and then rounding the corner to the back door. It was exquisite. Lifting the latch, we'd step into the passage, where Mrs Newton was nearly always running up and down between the Big Room and the Bar with a tray full of glasses or wet rings, red-faced but in control.

'Take off your coats, and come on up!'

There would be a burst of noise as you turned the brass knob, opened the door and squeezed your way in. People everywhere. The same old ones, about fifteen to twenty of them, never older, always old, all happy. Mrs Newton's 'specials'.

Sarah and Harry Newton kept the Swan. He looked after a bit of farming on the side, and she kept a cool eye and head on the business, standing no nonsense from anyone and occasionally treating the good customers. She was a stout little person, an excellent cook Mother said, who made her pastry with the lard from the pigs they killed, and you couldn't fault it, couldn't compete. On Boxing Night her sister Florrie Basham and her husband Alfie, and their daughters Clara and Sarah were always there too.

Alfie Basham sat by the fire, by the polished brass fender and poker and tongs and brush, on the little red velvet button chair which just fitted him. He was a short man, and became redder and hotter and more shiny and happy as the evening wore on. He would laugh and mop himself, and his watch-chain tugged and winked across his tight little waistcoat.

We rarely, if ever, saw this room throughout the rest of the year. Its sole purpose seemed to be for now, this one night of jollity, this highlight of happiness and singing and laughing and eating and banter. I doubt if the conversation changed much from year to year, for nothing much happened and the same old memories would be gone over again and again. And the room never changed. Along the wall by the door to the passage was the red plush sofa with its curly back and bolsters at each end. Opposite the fireplace, between the passage and the street, stood the long, heavy sideboard with a mirror at its back. Next to it by the window was the upright piano, and in the middle of the room stood the large table which later on would be laid for supper, but which for now was used for putting glasses on – beer, ginger beer, sherry, gin, port-and-lemons. And the voices rose. The Newtons were generous. 'What'll you have?' 'How's your glass?' Then someone would say, 'Give us a tune, Edie!' 'Where do flies go in the Winter time!' 'Oh, play "In a Monastery Garden" Edie!' 'What about "She was only a beautiful picture... la la la la la la la la... IN A BEAUTIFUL GOLDEN FRAME."'

'Wait till I can find the music,' Mother

would say, half frightened, half smiling with pleasure.

After a tentative start – 'I'm a bit rusty,' she'd say – it would begin, this party I so looked forward to. They sang, swaying to and fro on their seats. 'What about...?' 'Have you got...?' And so there would be 'Lily of Laguna', 'If you were the only girl in the world', 'Daisy', 'After the ball was over...' 'Who were you with last night?' ... 'Tipperary...' and on it went. Wonderful. And Mother sat and played and played, worth her weight in gold.

Some time later, Florrie and another woman would clear the table and lay it with a big white cloth that puffed a draught into your face. With straight backs they'd lean and flatten it, and smooth it, and then came the knives and forks; the big, tall cruets with vinegar, mustard, salt and pepper; the piles of plates; the dishes of butter; and the bread-boards with big Coburg or twist loaves that Grandad had made. I was allowed to carry the celery – crisp, virginal stuff – from the cold, cold kitchen and the chatter of the women there to the table, now made immense because the men had opened it out. It all appeared – the home-cured ham at one end, carved by Mr Porter, such a big man, who came from London; the great turkey at the other end (cooked by Grandad in the bakehouse on Christmas morning with the many others brought to him).

'Goo on!' Mr Newton would bellow as he carved it 'you can eat that!' as though the huge helpings were only enough to keep a bird alive.

At last the carving was done, and the knives raised. Someone would shout 'To Sal!' and down would go some fair swigs. Then she always said something which ended with 'and bless you all,' her eyes watery and unhappily happy as was her way.

There were home-made pickles, beer and home-made wine to drink, and after all that came Mrs Newton's sherry trifle, jugs sprouting celery, plates of Cheddar and Stilton cheese, and others piled high with her special mince pies.

There was laughter and jokes and compliments, but Mrs Newton's eye remained steadfast and watchful for her guests, a little stern with concentration, secretly savouring the success of it all. The noise was most of it. When I'd finished eating I was allowed to go under the table into the cool and look at the ladies' shoes, trying to guess which feet belonged to whom; and if Grandad had a wishbone he'd hand it down to me.

Mr Porter was large and red and important, and I thought he must be *the* Mr Porter whom you asked whatever should you do in the song, though I never knew the connection between him and Mr and Mrs

Newton. He used to bring two friends – Mabel and Flossie – down from London with him. All three of them spent most of the evening until supper down in the Tap Room. But after supper, Mabel was the star we all waited for. She had sparkling eyes, vivacity, a great jet-black bun in the nape of her neck, and high cheek-bones with a spot of rouge on each of them. I loved Mabel. I'd sit in my white ankle socks, on someone's knee while they turned themselves this way and that to talk, or reach a glass, oblivious of me as I was of them, waiting for Mabel to dress up and sing. But first the table had to be cleared and pushed back. The open door to the passage let in a welcome, icy, draught and old Peter would bank the fire.

At last she came in her tail coat with top hat and cane to do her 'Burlington Bertie' act. 'Quiet!' said somebody – and everyone sat still. Mother played the piano and Mabel, slim and dark, sang and strutted up and down in front of the fire. It had begun. It was heaven! Oh, it was wonderful!

But down in the Tap Room was Flossie, always on her own. She was blonde and not slim, and always wore a lovely long black dress, and her nails were the colour of wet radishes. She never joined the rest of us. Whenever I passed the open door of the Tap Room on my way to the lavatory up the stairs I could see her just sitting there with a glass, a little glass, and that looked beautiful and elegant too. But she always looked unhappily beautiful, even when talking to Mr Porter. And I never understood why she wore a long dress. It made her so romantic for me, but she didn't belong somehow. *We* always wore warm things.

After Mabel's act came 'Little Brown Jug' and 'Knees Up Mother Brown,' and nearly everyone joined in. As the night wore on, the singing became more and more halting, as fewer and fewer songs were remembered. When I got very tired, really tired, too tired, I could go to sleep on the red velvet sofa with the bolsters (I suppose it was plush, but to me it was velvet). And I'd sleep, sort of, then wake, and sleep again.

'Fred, the child's tired, we must go home!'

'What's that, me old beauty?' Grandad or Uncle, sounding very calm and relaxed. 'You tired? But you don't want to go home yet, do you?'

Of course I didn't. This was my night too!

'Oh, Fred ...!'

'I'll just finish this, then we'll go.'

We never did, of course.

Tired old bodies would make room for themselves next to me. A coat or cardigan would be laid over me. Mother would still be playing, but now her voice rose above the rest. The cold draught came more often through the door. When I opened my eyes, the light seemed flat and the room was much emptier.

Home we'd go at last, little old Billy Orbell carrying me in his arms, feeling with his feet for the kerb. Gran saying sharply 'Fred? Fred! Where are you, Fred? We're over here. Mind the wall!'

'Coming, dear.'

Then Gran and Mother would go ahead. It was such a tradition I didn't have to be fully awake to know it.

'Where's Charles?'

In the end, everybody got inside, and Mr Orbell went on his way. All that remained was the feeling that all had been accomplished, and how lovely it had been, and how I couldn't wait for the next time.

And upstairs, between the cotton sheets, our hot water bottles were but pale ghosts of themselves.

Dorie and Her Parents

Dorie and I had stared, or glared, at each other from our pram days, or so we were told, and the first row we had – just one of many – was when I lent her my tricycle to ride outside the shop, on the pavement between us and the butcher's. Round and round she went, as I had been doing, when all of a sudden, what did she do? She very deliberately drove the front wheel over my foot. I shrieked. My fury was immediate and immense.

'Say you're sorry,' I shouted.

All she did was go on round and call back over her shoulder, 'I'm not!'

It would be perfectly true to say that Dorie was the first person to dumbfound me.

And yet, on the whole, we were pretty inseparable, for most of the 'we's I write mean 'Dorie and me'.

We had both started at the village school at about the age of three or four, but I don't remember that we did things together until we were a bit older. At that time the Crick family lived just round the corner of the Post Office in the first of three cottages at the top of Nethergate Street. Mrs Crick always made me feel as welcome as if it was my home too, and it was there, sitting under the kitchen table, that we wrote our first plays. What Dorie's was about I don't remember. Mine had talking saucepans in it, and as we wrote we stuffed ourselves with a packet of greasy chips bought from the Fish and Chip Shop or van. Until a terrible queasiness overtook us – me, anyway – and for a long time afterwards the sight or thought of a grey aluminium saucepan could turn my stomach as quick as a wink.

Shortly after that, the family moved to the small house beside the cemetery driveway. Dorie's father worked next door for her grandfather, Mr Willis, delivering coal. On Sunday evenings he often cycled to villages around as a lay-preacher, chirpy as a grasshopper in all weathers. Staunch Congregationalists they were, pillars of the Chapel in that the whole family – grandfather and grandmother, great aunt, uncles and aunts, the whole lot of them – sang or played the organ, and attended both morning and evening services. No doubt we passed them on Sunday evenings bent on the earthly pleasures of the Swan. The great grandmother who had reached a hundred years had perhaps benefitted from that life of hardy discipline and abstinence.

Dorie was not allowed out to play on Sundays. Sunday was a day of clean shoes, washed hair, a hymn book and the walk to Chapel and back twice. One of her great aunts lived in Church Street, next to Mrs Wiffen's Library on the corner opposite the Bell, and used to read Improving Stories to us while we sat on the floor. She would wait until we were still, then rest her small black-booted feet under her long black skirt on a low embroidered stool, open the book in her mittened hands and begin. She had a quiet, slightly cracked, voice. And I liked particularly the way her teeth clicked very neatly and without fail, at the end of each sentence. Then she would lend us books such as 'The Little Match Girl' and we used to read them all, or nearly so. But they were sad, with Good Ladies in them, and even better children who died, and they palled. But none of that happened on Sundays, either.

When the Cricks moved, theirs was the house I came to know best, other than our own, and in earlier times, the Betts'. It was a three-up, three-down, with a bucket privy in the corner of the back garden. In spring, the garden was awash with the clean smell of wallflowers, dark blood-red, and yellow and speckled ones. Even now, a glass vase of them, some petals dropped and shrunken at its base, brings back their window-sill for me, and I see again their living room with the kitchen beyond full of the early evening sunlight. There Mr Crick washed himself after work, braces hanging down, his glasses put by the enamel bowl in which he first washed his face, then his neck, then his forearms. These he stood by turn in the bowl and pushed the grey, soapy water up and down with the other encircling hand. Drying himself on the towel behind the door, he'd listen to the news before stepping over the high wooden step in his big working boots to come and have his tea. He seemed to walk slightly lame in those enormous boots, and was somewhat bent after years of carrying on his back heavy sacks of coal.

But he was a strong, spare, man, not one to give in to weakness or illness, determined nothing should defeat him. He was a fighter, a socialist who read the Daily Herald; he held firm opinions and always spoke rather loudly, eager to be heard, giving freely of his thoughts to all and sundry, while Mrs Crick listened attentively, weighing up what he said, perhaps agreeing, sometimes quietly countering his remarks, or just being amused.

After tea, when it was fine and the right time of year, he would take his spade or fork or hoe, or all three balanced on the wheelbarrow, and go up the garden next door for an hour or so, and either gloat or bemoan on his return. When we were young we were given jam jars of salt water, and sent up to the cabbages to pick off the caterpillars and drop them into the water. Next door had a very large garden that was shared out among others rather like allotments. Squared off by narrow grass paths, the different sections were laid out and tended, and produced all and more that a family could want in the way of potatoes, carrots, beet, beans, marrows, cabbages and peas. In summer there were lettuces and cucumbers and tomatoes. Much was given away of course to those who, like us, had no garden, while the prize gems were brought on and polished and placed proudly on show at the annual Flower Show, or given to the Church or Chapel at Harvest Festival.

Henry Crick revelled in tomes of comparative theology and suchlike weighty matters. When the travelling library called at the school he would be one of the first to probe along the shelves with loud exclamations, and then stagger gleefully back home in his heavy boots like a dog with juicy bones. As Dorie grew up the two of them jousted their opinions against one another with great relish, for they were very alike. He was an excitable man, loud and voluble, cheerful, yet perhaps lacking sensitivity. On Sundays his hair was combed and pressed close to his head, and his big boots were replaced by a lighter pair. He lived his life with no apparent need of friends – and there were few, if any, with his interests and intellectual ability in Clare – and yet he enjoyed himself hugely. His pipe, work, garden and the scriptures were enough, plus, of course, his family, the Library and his Sunday work. After the War he was able to afford a moped to take him to the outlying chapels. The two of them made a strange combination, but it was his pride and joy, and saved his energy after work that must have been harder and harder the older he became.

Dorie's mother was older than her husband by quite a few years. A small, narrow woman with wiry grey hair in a bun just below the crown of her head. Her worn, rough hands were always searching for escaping pins and replacing them, sweeping back the uncaught strands. All morning she wore her cross-over overall, and on her thin legs the grey stockings inevitably slipped into folds around her ankles. She wouldn't know, couldn't see, but they were part of her appearance. Her spectacles were very thick and round and she used her hands a lot, to feel things with. If she picked up a book or paper, she had to hold it next to her face, her spectacles lifted a little, to see anything of what was written. She often had to take pails up the next door yard to the pump by the big black cones of coal, and bring them back one at a time, full of water. And her small, thin, triangular face had, not surprisingly, a firm, if not determined, pointed chin.

Her special way of walking was 'ten to two' and, having changed her shoes for a more respectable pair – though possibly of identical style, or perhaps button-across ones – she would put on her hat and coat, take her brown handbag and the shopping basket, and go down to Lufkin's the grocers most afternoons, and sometimes to the Post Office too, and here and there, and be back again in time to get the tea.

Saturday dinner time was the main meal of the week end and, as with us, it began with Yorkshire pudding and gravy from the meat that was to follow. All was cooked in the black cast-iron range in the living room, whose fire was always alight, and where a great big black velvety kettle sat singing gently in the corner. Mrs Crick would crouch down in front of it, in her grey wrinkled stockings, her back straight, her hands carefully seeking things that should be brought out and tested and turned.

When she stood, which was often, I remember now that her face was usually turned a little to one side, with one hand either on the table or a chair back. She stood a lot, and certainly thought a lot. I doubt if anyone had ever heard her voice raised. What she said was carefully to the point, always careful never to be hurtful, ready to be fair, full of her thoughtful working-out. Her opinions were broached tentatively but firmly and, if rejected, then she tucked them quietly back again for another time.

But Dorie's parents accepted me, and I was almost one of them and spent so much of my time there, particularly at tea time. I loved Mrs Crick's blackcurrant jam, which was nearly solid with fruit and crunchy with sugar; a gorgeous colour on glossy yellow butter, spread on thick slices of white bread with slightly blackened, sweet, edges. Once her husband had gone up the garden, then Mrs Crick might take some mending or knitting and go and sit with her family next door. As far as I know, she rarely went anywhere except there, or to visit her aunt next to Mrs Wiffen, and to Chapel and the shops, and to the east coast for an annual week's holiday when that became possible and affordable.

Occasionally, I was allowed to stay the night, which was a great event. I had the spare room at the front, next to Dorie's, and slept on the feather mattress in the big bed which nearly filled the little room. The floor sloped and creaked, and you had to kneel down to look out of the window, and could very nearly touch the tops of passers-bys' heads, let alone hear most of what they were saying. The Church clock across the road struck the quarters all day and through the night, and was like a huge guardian looking after us. There was a washstand, and we washed in the morning in the still-warm water from our hot water bottles. And had fried bread and bacon for breakfast.

It was like a second home for me. And yet, it lacked the smack of otherness, looseness, weakness perhaps, and the coming and going of the outside world with its foibles and problems. Their small house was a tight little bastion against such things, whereas ours had many draught holes through which miseries could blow and settle.

Games

In Dorie's house, too, there were always snippets of material left over from her Aunt Nellie's dress-making, from which we cut out oblongs of the right length, folded them in half, and cut half-moons for head-holes. These then slipped over our little celluloid dolls' heads, and with a piece of wool round their waists their new dresses were complete. Any unused snippets of material were never wasted: they came in for rag rugs which most houses had, and which wore and wore.

Just as we couldn't resist collecting things like spanking-new shiny 'conkers' or the brilliant red leaves of creepers with which we stuffed our dolls' prams full to over-flowing, nor could we resist intriguing hiding places to put things in. And the red brick wall going up to the Almshouses was just the job for that. The bricks had begun to crumble in places, and thin biscuity edges hid tiny caves and crevasses in which to stow small treasures that we found on our wanderings, perhaps a pretty pebble, or a small special flower head, or a specially good chunk of chalk you could mark things with. It worked the other way round too: some little hiding places were so perfect and exciting we had to go and find something immediately to put in them. Whatever we saw and loved we owned, just as we loved and 'owned' the wall, for it *was* our wall in that it played such a strong part in our lives, and contained so much else that we prized.

One day, having two really good pieces of chalk, we were moved to create our first public art work, and the blank wall of the slaughterhouse in the Lane was just right for that. Carefully we drew what we liked best: pretty ladies with long curly hair, very triangular skirts and handbags. To finish off, we gave them two circles up top with dots inside. Our work complete, and the chalk nearly used up, we went on our way to see to the next thing that needed doing.

But Mr Hurry the butcher was not pleased at all, as we learned soon enough. In fact he was very, very cross indeed, and even our mothers seemed to be as well. We were given a pail full of soapy water and two scrubbing brushes and had to stand there and scrub and scrub until every bit of our ladies had gone. The indignity of it all was hard to bear, so we didn't feel much like doing it again. Not there, anyway.

When we were much older, and when there was nothing to do but get out of the house for we were in the way, and the weather was too bad for anything else, we could spend the time standing in one of the Town Hall porches searching the whole Market Hill for things we had never noticed before. It may have been a chimney stack with a brick missing, the shape of a window or doorway, the way something in a house was not as you would have expected from the rest of it, some detail of pattern – there was always something to keep us on our toes. I think it must have grown out of games of 'I Spy' we had played there earlier, or even from those series of little pictures you had to compare to find out how they differed. Whatever, it was in some ways a very satisfying way of passing the time, and there was always something new to find.

On the other hand, for a supposedly country child I, for one, was sorely ignorant of the names of birds or trees, apart from the obvious ones, of course. What was around us was there, had its shape and colour and characteristics, was familiar, and looked like this at certain times and that at others. Things came and went, and always would. One knew them by sight, and names seemed unnecessary. When 'that' happened, then so would something else. But the wild dog roses that grew on the Gun Hill facing the Station, and on the hill opposite, were a special, favourite, happening. So pretty, so pink, their stamens so yellow, just like the Alexandra roses we bought each year.

'You must never take sweets from a stranger,' Mother had said to me, more than once. Once, down by the Station, before you came to the wild roses, there was an old man all overgrown with hair, and he offered us sweets, and the bag he held was so sticky and dirty-looking we couldn't have fancied them anyway. We hadn't felt threatened either. Mother had never told me *why* one should never take such offerings, but she need not have worried in that one and only case.

Station Road held other delights, for on the waste ground next to the Thompsons' flint house there was a throwaway dump, and an old abandoned car. Rummaging on the dump produced the most desirable objects – perhaps a little mirror, a pretty tin box, even a handbag or a purse, and once we found a real powder compact that

88

snapped properly to. Then we could sit in the car afterwards and pretend to be grown-ups going out for the day. Needless to say, we were never allowed to keep our treasures.

Clare People

Auntie Hilda

Our house, as you may have gathered, was a somewhat secular abode. It was Auntie Hilda Betts from next door who took me by the hand at Easter time each year to see the Magic Lantern show of the Holy Land in the Church. The clicking machine showed slides of a yellow country which did not mean much to me, but I knew that to her they were of immense worth – and this, to me very beautiful, lady with high cheek bones, in hat and gloves wanted me to see them too, and so I did. But after a while my eyes would wander. It was enough just to be there, in the faint light with the dark height of the nave above us, sitting beside her, sensing the reverence and specialness she felt.

Her parents' house was thin and tall, three rooms on top of each other and a kitchen pushed out the back. Here we would link arms, she and I, and prance up and down while we sang 'Sally Broke the Jam Pot, the Jam Pot, the Jam Pot...' until we collapsed with laughing, quite exhausted. Then we would climb the stairs to her room, the top one, as high as a rook's nest it seemed, from where you could peer down one way across the Market Hill, and the other way over roofs and into back yards. It was a very special place, reached by a cupboard stair from their front room downstairs, first to her parents' bedroom and then by another door, and yet another staircase to this, her own. It contained her wide-brimmed hats and long necklaces, which I was allowed to try on while sitting on the scratchy black sofa in front of the back window. And here were scent bottles and smelly hankies and lavender bags as well. What we talked about I really do not remember, but it could have been about angels which we both strongly believed in. Or perhaps Jesus, for she was very religious. Some said she was a little bit touched that way, but if so, then it made her the most good person I had ever known. She was not always at home. She came sometimes, and sometimes she was 'away'. Where that was, I never knew and it didn't matter because when she came back she was always the same, and as soon as she could, she came round to see us.

'Edie, dear,' she would say to Mother in her timorous voice, 'I have just brought you this.'

And more often than not there would be

something for Gran as well, and even for me.

'Oh, my dear, you shouldn't have,' Mother would say as Hilda stood there, tall and thin and nervously waiting for her small presents to be opened. Perhaps a small bottle of lavender water tied with ribbon for Gran, a pretty scarf for Mother, and once she gave me a necklace of tiny beads with little bead-people holding hands at the front. In fact, if the truth be told, she spoiled me, and yet she seemed to love it as much as I did.

One Christmas morning a large brown paper package stood on the shop counter. It was for me from Auntie Hilda, for her large, whirly writing was quite unmistakable. Inside was a blue painted wooden cot with a proper let-down side, and lying in it was the biggest celluloid doll you could imagine. It was a baby boy, called Robin apparently, and came complete with a blue crocheted top and shorts, and even had underwear. He also had a bottle which fitted into a hole in his lips, but I was relieved that it really didn't do anything. Anyway, he was a most accommodating sort of person, for he allowed Teddy and Dinah to take enormous liberties with his cot while he looked happy wherever he was. He had a very giving nature. Dear Auntie Hilda, she liked to give the best, as she was doing when she gave me the jointed French doll. She was so vulnerable. Somewhere I still have the only Prayer Book I ever owned: another present from her.

And to me, no one was more elegant. She took care of her appearance. She used scent and powder, and always had a lace handkerchief and wore gloves and frocks. She never altered, and remained loving and giving.

Her parents seemed to be much older than Gran and Grandad, although they couldn't have been much older, if at all. Mr Betts was tall and thin, with a drooping white moustache and deep-set eyes. His wife was small and dressed a little like Dorie's Great Aunt. I *think* Mr Betts had worked at the butcher's until he retired, but I can't be sure. But I do know that I loved having dinner with him and his wife for their plates had a faded Prussian Blue pattern on them and their wooden-handled forks gave the food a very special taste of fried bacon. When I mentioned this to Gran she said it was because they weren't cleaned properly, and I thought that to be strangely disloyal of her.

When I went to visit one day – and this is all well before the War – Mrs Betts was cutting her corns by the fire in the front room. She'd been soaking her foot in an enamel basin and now it was on a small round stool in front of her. In her hand she had the sort of razor Grandad used when he was shaving. She was speaking to me as she bent over, but after one glance I concentrated on the glass prisms on the mantelpiece and was careful never to return at a time when I thought she might be doing that...

But their home, too, was a place where I could come and go as I wished, another extension of my own. It faded, though, as I grew older and ceased to need or even value what they, in my need, had given me. As the years had gone on, Auntie Hilda's visits home became less and less frequent and eventually they stopped, and she disappeared from our lives like a tall, thin, sad wraith, and nobody knew what became of her. Or if they did, they did not tell me. Auntie Hilda was very special.

The Parkers

Next door to the Betts lived the Parkers. That was different. The feel of the shop – they sold shoes – was one of GO. Once inside, it always looked a little empty and dark, and most of the shelves were curtained, but a ready head would pop through at door-handle level from the inner room, to see who'd come in. Sometimes it would be Mrs Parker who served, searching for shiny black Wellingtons or whatever else we needed; sometimes it would be her daughter Joyce.

They both wore their black hair in buns under brightly crocheted pull-ons and dressed alike in cross-over aprons. Straight-backed, straight-necked, chin tucked in, Joyce was full of energy and somewhat indelicate good nature. She was as brisk as a hailstorm, a short, staccato little person who never minced her words. A spade was a spade, and if she felt like swearing, she swore, in broadest Suffolk and all. She was uncompromising, dominant, fierce even, and her dark eyes didn't miss a thing. Her laugh could be heard over roof-tops and through walls, and so could her curses too.

But under the mannerisms was hidden Joyce's kindness, and when I was a baby she would take me for a night or two to give Mother a break.

'Cry?' I'd hear her say later, in company. 'She'd holler her head off all night long. You couldn't do a thing with her! Ain't that right, Edie?'

And turning to me, she would say with mock fierceness and a shake of the head: 'Yew little ol' devil, yew!' And that was her way of showing affection.

She wouldn't stand any nonsense though, and when I was about five or six, or perhaps even seven, I'd be sent round to Joyce with my knitting or embroidery or colouring or reading books, and sit and be good. Their living room next to the shop bloomed with embroidered flowers, on cushions and antimacassars and a stool and the fire-screen used in summer. The brass and copper all gleamed and the rooms were spotless – all thanks to Joyce and her mother's industry. She taught Sunday School at Chapel, and kept the discipline at home too. I still have the small book she gave me, with pictures on each page illustrating the moral tales beneath them. It bears the inscription: 'Annie Crow, 1888.' I had to read those stories to myself sometimes while I was in their house and she was busy.

Mr Parker was in the building trade. He too was small, and went by the name of Old Strutt because of the way he walked, I thought. Some said you had to watch him.

The Parkers' back yard was long and narrow, one of the very few that gave onto the High Street at the far end, through locked gates. From the back of their house ran a long line of sheds roofed in corrugated iron that seemed to be crammed with a huge amount of things, and sometimes even kittens. I couldn't begin to describe it, for it never interested me apart from the kittens, but was what I suppose we would have called junk. Though during the war Strutt sometimes had particular little 'treasures' which he was willing to let you have at a price. He gave me a little object once, and I never did find out what to do with it, and he didn't seem to know either. It was made of silvery metal, four or five inches long, and boat-shaped, with a mouthpiece and a round hole half way along it. I kept it because I felt I should, and one day would understand it. But I never did. Even though I tried blowing on it, and through it, it never spoke or proclaimed itself.

The Parkers had connections in London, and sometimes a friend or two would come and stay with them, and we got to know them slightly. Sometimes Joyce had something which she thought Mother might like to buy, and one day she came with a pair of high-heeled green suede lace-up shoes. Never had we seen shoes like them. Mother tried them on then and there, and of course fell in love with them. Sadly, she did not have anywhere much to go in them, but she bought them and wore them all the same.

Much later on, when Joyce was a very old lady in her eighties, living alone in the big house in Nethergate Street which her family had moved into many years earlier, my husband and I went to visit her. We had tried once or twice before but there had never been an answer. This time, as we stood on the steps by the front door, tentatively wondering whether she would be there, whether we would be welcome, someone knocked on the window trying to catch our attention. A young woman was pointing to the side gate.

I knew from that moment that Joyce had certainly not changed.

We went through the gate, closing it carefully behind us, and the young visiting nurse – for that is what she was – opened the side door. We told her who we were, and waited for her to come back.

'Come through,' she said, and led us through the small kitchen to the room at the front.

And there she sat, looking so much smaller than I remembered; but the eyes, they were the same Joyce-eyes, and for an instant she sat quite still, just looking at me. Then out it came, the familiar voice, a bit older, not quite so Suffolky as it had once been.

'How you do look like your dear Mother!'

I smiled. I could have hugged her.

Nothing for it, there had to be a glass of sherry all round. Could we help? No. She got herself up from the chair, and I saw how her legs seemed to be terribly swollen. She bustled slowly around to find four glasses, and then the bottle. And as I had expected, the room was full of furniture and other things she liked, and had collected to appease the magpie streak that ran through her father too. All looked neat and clean as a whistle. It was like coming home after light-years of travel. Well could I believe the vague rumour that the whole house was a veritable treasure trove, all dusted and polished and gleaming: that was Joyce all over.

We talked, and I mentioned Mother, then in her ninety-eighth year. 'Ah, is Edie still alive then? Do give her my love,' she added sadly. And then she began remembering all those days long gone, and Mother and Gran, and the hard life they'd had. As I listened I pictured my mother, now old and frail, and felt proud of the way she had battled through, sustained many a time by that wicked little sense of humour she had, and a willingness to go for a bit of fun – which popped up so very rarely in her life. Then Joyce spoke about her own late marriage, and how she had survived. She had always been indomitable, and here she was, living in this grand house, but just the same as ever. No side, and a spade still a spade.

In my mind I planned to go back with photos of Mother on both her ninetieth and ninety-fifth birthdays, and to enjoy hearing Joyce once more pour out her memories, to be a sort of meeting point for those two old ladies at the end of their lives. But I left it too late, and never saw her again. One thing I know for sure: how the never-failing generous side of her nature, and her pride, would have revelled mightily in being able to leave one million pounds to the West Suffolk Hospital on her death.

And, as someone said, she'd go to heaven

with a duster in her pocket, too.

Miss Ager

The house next door to the Parkers was where Miss Ager lived with her parents, and was not one I visited. Later on, Miss Ager was to teach Dorie and me in the school, and read books to the class sitting on the empty desk in front of me, her polished brown shoes on the chair seat. One story we most particularly loved was of a young boy hiding in an ivy-covered ruin from the Roman soldiers. Because of her commitment – though Dorie was naturally gifted and clever – we both got scholarships to the local girls' High School in Sudbury. Miss Ager was unlike the other teachers in that nothing about her stood out. She was middle-aged, with a grey bun, unexciting to look at, but had stickability and a steadfast devotion to her work and her 8, 9 and 10-year old pupils, of whom, I suppose, there were about 20. She wasn't really easy to like and went under the name of Aggie – but none the less, when it came to the crunch, you respected her.

The Muggs

On the corner, just beyond the Agers' big

gates which had been used for horses and carriages when the house was still the old Temperance Hotel, lived Mr and Mrs Mugg and their daughter Florence. He was a cobbler, and his wife and daughter kept the tiny shoe shop on the very corner itself – where, later on in the war, huge tanks rumbling through Clare in the night, had to slow down and edge their way round the bend.

Whereas the Parkers' shop was brusque and full of go and gossip, here in the Muggs' it was dark and quiet and slow, and very soothing. We usually got our Christmas slippers there, and sometimes my brown leather sandals with crepe soles as well. Florence too was quiet and slow, a pale girl almost without colour, who must have suffered from some kind of allergy for she always seemed to have a cold which made her nose red, and gave her the only colour she had in her face. Mrs Mugg was thin and quiet too. They were Plymouth Brethren, and kept themselves very much to themselves.

Mr Mugg's workshop was immediately after the Agers' gateway, looking down Station Road. Over the top of the low curtain, it was possible to catch his eye, and if he nodded that meant that I could go in. I always had to sit and be good. He rarely talked to me as he sat in a leather apron crouched over a sole or a heel on a smooth steel mould which gleamed like grey satin, for his mouth was usually pursed over a row of nails. Beside him on the floor was a steadily growing pile of curly leather off-cuts from soles and heels, which he ran round neatly with a knife, trimming them exactly. The nails were placed on the leather by his finger and thumb and tapped in quickly and evenly. Half-moon shaped blakeys were sometimes put onto heels to give them extra wear. I liked his big magnet which picked up long, dangling, chains of grey nails with a dull sheen, pulled and held them fast, and the higher you held it the thinner the chains became. They had their own grey-metal smell, just as the pungent leather had its own. After a while I would go, sensing a welcome about to be out-stayed.

Miss Twitchett

The only other person who held their mouth pursed in that way was Miss Twitchett the dressmaker who lived at the top of Station Road in the first of the row of red brick cottages. She did that with pins, in her front room at fittings. First with the waist, then the sleeves and collar, and then with the hem while I stood on the table. She was so clever she hardly ever pricked, and Mother and she would decide exactly what was to be what.

She was so quiet and patient, and I loved going to her.

Miss Tuffin and Susie Stiff

The first shop round the corner after the Muggs' was Miss Bessie Tuffin's fish shop. Nowadays we are used to seeing displays of fish in shop windows, but I don't remember there being much on show in Miss Tuffin's. Although there was always plenty inside, in boxes, on the cool brick floor. One stepped down into her white-washed room and there would be glossy brown-and-gold kippers, gold-and-silver bloaters, silvery red-eyed fat herrings, yellow haddock, pans of little dark winkles with their half-pint measures sitting in them, pink shrimps and slippery sprats, glistening dabs and plaice and sole. She would appear from the back with a little anxious smile, eager to please, and with red, rough, sore-looking hands that always seemed to be comforting each other.

She was short, and had darkish-grey frizzy hair worn high at the back, with a very crinkly fringe over her eyes. If you asked for something not in the shop she would disappear again, for what always seemed an awfully long time, to her store in the yard. It must have been tiny. For when we lived later in the Agers' house you could see almost everything, but not into Bessie Tuffin's back yard. You could only smell it a bit.

Her fish was as fresh as could be, coming straight from Lowestoft or Yarmouth at dawn each morning, and it tasted wonderful. We mostly had her Yarmouth bloaters, or kippers, or herrings with big fat roes at breakfast. We didn't go in for white fish. Grandfather also loved winkles and I learned to like them as well, enjoying the ritual of removing their heads and winkling them out with a pin.

Next to Miss Tuffin lived Susie Stiff who, with her sister, kept the sweet shop on the corner of the High Street. As I have said, Grandad sold sweets too, but only loose ones in jars, whereas Susie Stiff sold lovely different ones, all shapes and sizes and colours, and in different packages with their special names. You could choose this or that or something else to make up a penny's worth. She had yellow triangular packets of sherbet with either a liquorice tube to suck it through or a sticky dab to suck it off; liquorice coils with an aniseed ball in the middle; liquorice pipes; lollipops; brittle toffee pieces that made it impossible to talk; jelly babies; toffee bars to suck and bend and chew; white chocolate bars. And of course she had jars of Spanish Comforts and pear drops and acid drops and butterscotch and allsorts and humbugs – masses of them, on the shelves behind. Miss Stiff was large and red-faced, well corsetted and very strict. We used to spend a long time outside deciding what to buy for a penny, or sometimes a ha'penny, because woe betide you if you didn't know by the time you went in, or had forgotten.

Mr Pickworth and the Ambrosinis

Shortly before the war began, the Muggs' house took on a split personality for me. They let the room over the workshop to a dentist who came every Monday morning from Glemsford. For a time I had to be treated by him every week and this I dreaded and disliked from the bottom of my soul. Up until then it had only been the infrequent inspection and treatment by the visiting school dentist. Now I had gingivitis, and the treatment of the time was for my gums to be lanced. It was a regular, painful feature of my life, impossible to avoid. Even for Mother, Sunday nights became a trial.

It did not matter that Mr Pickworth looked so well turned-out and clean in his dapper grey suit with always a flower in his button hole, and his neat, pointed grey-white goatee beard. Normally I would have been delighted to watch such an unusual-looking person. But he was precisely the one thing I wished to blot out from life altogether, without being able to, he and the smell and the chair and the silver hooks and prongs and tongs.

Yet another transformation took place in the Muggs' house once the war had started. A dark-haired, comfortably-covered lady and gentleman called Mr and Mrs Ambrosini arrived with their son Carlo. They spoke a special and very interesting English, and were so warm and friendly. Carlo and I became great friends. He was my age, nine, and round, with tight, short grey trousers, and was always so well wrapped up except for his knees. And happy, and laughing and kind. On those dreadful Monday mornings it was always Carlo who came and talked to me beforehand, as Mother and I sat and waited in that upstairs back room that was his and his parents' bed-sitting room for the rest of the week. He would wait for me, and then we would go down to Mr Mugg and play quietly with his magnet and nails.

We would also play for hours with dinky cars and lorries in the pile of sand left by workmen in our yard, making roads and bridges and tunnels. Or we would play with playing cards, or jigsaw puzzles or board games. Or, wrapped up in our big winter scarves, we would go exploring. Even with Dorie sometimes. And there was never any doubt, any second thought, that Carlo would be privy to any of our secret or special places. If he was interested that is. Just occasionally he might lack a little enthusiasm, but was always polite. Mr and Mrs Ambrosini were not always there and sometimes he went away too. Perhaps he was only there in the holidays. Yet I do know that news of his coming was something to savour and look forward to with real pleasure. Gradually his visits became more and more rare and eventually stopped altogether. But by then we were in our early teens, and life and our interests had changed once again. I have often wondered about that odd mixture – the Plymouth Brethren and the little Italian family – but we didn't think at all about it then.

Mr Bruce

Across the Market Hill from us, behind the War Memorial, was a narrow house with a pointed gable in the middle of which was a large clock face. Here Mr Bruce kept his jeweller's shop, though to tell the truth he mainly mended clocks and watches and looked after the Church clock. If you went up the steps and through the door, there he would be, a wiry little man with wire-rimmed spectacles and a thin face, sitting behind the counter bent over the workings of something or other. It was a tiny shop, and fitted him snugly. He arrived just before nine o'clock each morning on his bicycle, in a three-piece suit, having come down the Ashen Road not far from the Bathing Place.

What we children liked most, of course, was to look into his high window at the array of rings and brooches and watches and decide what we would like to have most. By today's standards the choice was small and seldom altered, but this gave us the chance to change our minds next time the fancy took us. The sight of the sparkling jewels – and they must have been mostly rhinestones – lying on the black velvet in their boxes enchanted us. Some must have been there for years and years, so familiar they became to us: one was a butterfly brooch with different coloured stones in its wings. Not a favourite, it seemed, of anybody's, for it had been there as long as we could remember.

When each of us said, almost competitively, 'I'll have that!' it wasn't that we truly wanted it, for we knew we couldn't have any of them, and it didn't matter. They became ours for a brief moment through the glass, until we moved onto something else. But years later, looking down in the dark from an aeroplane onto the golden-silver chains of lights and the glittering brooches of towns and cities, I am back again looking into Mr Bruce's window, enthralled yet again by the enchantment of the contrast of sparkling lights and black velvet.

The Butchers

Across the Lane from us was Mr Hurry's butcher's shop, and further back towards the High Street was his slaughter house. Up and down the Lane was a constant coming and going, for it was a short cut for some to Lufkins the grocers and the haberdashery and the ironmongers', let alone the Post Office. Mr Scroggins was Mr Hurry's main assistant. A tall, mild-mannered man, kindly, with a ready smile and large red hands and forearms. He too went up and down the Lane in his long stained apron, carrying a large pail and sometimes a broom, when he wasn't serving in the shop.

The slaughterhouse, where the pigs squealed terribly, was on the right, a little way past the bakehouse. But we took little notice then. There were animals you stroked and played with, like our cat and dog, and there were animals that were good to eat. Nowadays I would be upset by those squealing pigs, but then we thought nothing of the sight of the clean, dripping, carcasses hanging there afterwards. Sheep too. And I can still hear the clank of the pail and the short rushing sounds the stiff

110

broom and water made when Mr Scroggins swept it all clean again.

Mr Hurry the butcher was both Hurry by name and Hurry by nature, Grandad always said. But his wife was quiet and short and slow with rheumatism, and it was always warm and comfortable in her clean cream-and-brown painted kitchen, where their hams and bacon matured. I liked to watch her prepare and fill and cover a steak and kidney pudding, and sometimes she asked me if I would like to come back when it was ready and have dinner with them; or help her dust upstairs; or go and get Dinah my doll and bring my piece of knitting too. Their house was calm and spacious and even a little grand compared with our hurly-burly. Perhaps they owned their house. We didn't. We paid rent and, quite possibly, a little haphazardly at times.

Mr Hurry's shop had tiles set in under his window, one tile with the head of a woolly sheep on it, and another with the head of a cow. Inside, all was spick and span with new sawdust on the floor each day, and a wide, well-scrubbed and slightly wavy counter in the middle. Fresh carcasses of beef and lamb or pork hung from a metal bar on the wall to the Lane. Joints hung on meat hooks over the side behind him, while offal and chops and suchlike were arranged neatly in the window. With a deft, quick flash of steel he would rasp a razor-sharp edge to his knife in no time at all, for he seemed to have an air of impatience about him, as though there was no time to waste before getting on to the next customer or job to be done. And indeed I am sure he was a busy man, for he also kept a small farm down at Bench Barn.

From him we had fat pork sausages which Gran boiled, and then we ate them cold for breakfast, cut in half lengthwise and skinned and eaten with mustard, mixed on our plates with a little vinegar. Or else cold pig's chitterlings crinkled and white and glistening in their own jelly, with salt and mustard. Sometimes there was half a cold sheep's head, the left-over from having it hot with caper sauce the day before, but now with some of the cheek and tongue and white of the eye still intact and sweet and more-ish; or cold sheep's brains. All these were favourites of ours, and so was the cold boiled belly pork, pink and white and delicious; and fried sweetbreads. From Mrs Perry's pork butcher's shop in Callis Street we had stiff, meaty pork cheeses, and there you could buy, for just a few pennies, her pork fritters – delicious crispy morsels left floating in the pans when she made the lard, scooped out, left to drain, and popped into paper bags.

The bread was always white, but the treat was Danuks. That was our name for the baked knobbles of dough cut off when the loaves were weighed before being moulded. Baked to a rich brown-black, still hot from the pre-breakfast batch, the butter melted immediately on the springy white crumb, and the crust was crunchy and sweet.

Our main meals during the week were stews, oxtails, steak and kidney pudding, bacon and onion pudding, or salt beef with carrots and dumplings in its broth. At the weekend we had a joint according to the season. Mother loved to cook. She did quite a lot even though she spent much of her time in the bakehouse too. It never occurred to us to have steak or such like. We had chops occasionally, but nothing could have been tastier or smelt better than what we ate anyway.

Before the war, it was Mr Scroggins who cleaned the pigs' intestines, turning them inside out, washing them, and then repeating it again and again, to make sure. Then they could become chitterlings. Who did the Newtons' I don't know: perhaps old Peter under the eye of Mrs Newton. It was hard work preparing a pig, using all but the squeak so as to waste nothing.

During the war, we had a pig, kept for us by old Peter, so we continued to get all the delicious bits and pieces. But as for the curing of hams, all that I knew was that women were not allowed near them. Something about them, it seemed, could 'turn' the meat and spoil it, particularly at certain times of the month. The hams and sides of bacon hung in the bakehouse, swathed in muslin against the flies, and were the entire responsibility of the men. Thinking back, and remembering Mother re-telling this, I have the feeling that she was thankful to be let off one more arduous task.

Cecil the Milkman

As I have said, Mr Hurry's butchers' shop was next to us on the other side of the Lane, and beyond it was the Orbell's garage. It wasn't so much a petrol garage as a mending one, I believe, and outside Mrs Orbell's front door in summer there were sometimes lettuces for sale, or a bunch of flowers, or some newly picked tomatoes, all for a few pence. By mid-afternoon the sun had gone round, and so the pavement was cool and the produce was just right for tea, when Cecil would arrive with the afternoon milk round.

He came round twice a day, in the pony cart, with milk from the Priory Farm in big churns. On each doorstep was a milk jug, carefully covered with a piece of muslin weighted with glass beads round the edge, to keep the flies out. He would stop the float, get down, go to each house in turn to fetch and fill the jug with the required amount – he could always tell from the size of the jug what that was – using the pint and half-pint measures which hung on long hooked handles on the side of the churns. He was the mildest of men, round-faced and quiet, and as reliable as the old church clock.

Sometimes we children made extra journeys to the farm to bring back milk in white enamel cans. The path skirted two sides of the Priory grounds, and the first part, next to the water meadows where there were cows and kingcups, was overhung with shadowy chestnuts with good branches for swinging on. The other part ran round the corner over a second white bridge and past a tall yew hedge with pretty orange-pink fruits in Autumn. But the last part was always a challenge for me because I was afraid of the geese and turkeys which came hissing and gobbling towards us once we had gone through the farmyard gate. It was always a great relief to be safely back on the path by the yew hedge again, though the cool, fresh, dainty cleanliness of the dairy had been worth the effort of getting there. On the way home we would take the lids off the milk cans and see who was best at swinging the can right round with a straight arm several times without spilling any. The worst only happened if your courage failed you!

Arthur Deeks the Tailor

Arthur cycled in each morning from Cavendish, his smooth face always genial whatever
the weather: he was always dressed for it,
and rather stylishly so. Arthur would always
have a smile for you when he dismounted at
the bottom of the Lane, even if the rain was
pouring off the front of his sou'wester. Even
if it dripped down to his trousers, neatly
nipped into their cycle clips. People mattered. His appearance mattered. He had self-
respect, and respected others'. His attire was
always appropriate, his shoes immaculately
polished, and even his rain-cape had a
certain dash about it.

He was such a friendly man, tall, bald, so
obliging, and called nearly everyone 'my
dear'. Some, of course, you couldn't. Mr
Hurry the butcher, for instance. I think it
really must have been only the females he
called 'my dear'. He was a bachelor, and
seemed to be a happy man though it is
impossible for me to say if he really was. He
was a dear man in any case, and I do not
believe that he knew what malice or anything like it was. He surprised me one day
when I was a grown woman by telling me
that he had been taken back stage to meet

Liz Taylor, and, 'my dear, what an event *that* was!' And yet, thinking about it, perhaps it was not so surprising. I was happy for him that he had excitements like that to keep him so smiling and pleased with life.

Susie Plum

Susie Plum lived in what must have been one of the smallest cottages, if not *the* smallest, in Clare. It was overgrown and stood behind a wooden garden gate down Cavendish Lane. When she arrived I have no idea, nor even where from. Perhaps she had always been there, but I don't think so. She was known by Mother as 'Poor Susie Plum' for her face was the ugliest one could imagine. She looked a bit like late portraits of Somerset Maugham, but even they lack the way her poor face was pulled from the top down. And none of it her fault, it seemed. For years earlier, who knows when, she had had what none of us really knew about – a face lift. Tragically, it had gone wrong, and left her for ever deformed. If you couldn't see her face, she had style and almost a touch of elegance. But when she turned, it took your breath away.

Though none of that prevented her having lots of visitors during the war. Soldiers went to her cottage to have their fortunes told (so

117

Mother said), and that made her very special in our eyes. And so she remains: someone with a doorway hung with roses and honeysuckle, who sits at a table in a tiny, shadowed room, gazing intently into a shining crystal ball. Round her neck hang the heavy beads she liked to wear, and her nails are always painted dark red.

Mr Skillings

Mr Skillings had his blacksmith's forge at the top of Cavendish Lane, opposite the side of the Bell, and just inside and to the right of the entrance to the Lee's yard. There a carthorse might be awaiting its turn, tapping and scraping its hooves on the cobbles. Inside it was all black and red, and we stayed by the opening for it was too busy to go in, and Mr Skillings did not welcome us. So I remember only the black and red, the noise of clanging metal, the hiss of steam, and the sight of him bent over in his leather apron with a hoof between his knees. There were bellows, and he had someone to help him.

When he grew old and his hair was white, his face was still handsome, with deep-set eyes and a drooping Kitchener moustache. He lived alone after his wife died, in another row of brick cottages down Station Road, next to the Bailey, and was one day found drowned in the shallow backwater by the railway.

Out into the World

Dancing lessons

Naturally enough Miss Amber Foster had red hair. She was a dancing teacher who gave lessons in the upstairs room leading off the back of the Half Moon. Here Mother brought me each week, and here I sat like the Rock of Gibraltar, implacable, a four-year old lump of obstinacy who 'resolutely wouldn't dance.' What I couldn't explain then was the embarrassment I felt at knowing none of the other children there, at feeling different from them, afraid to make mistakes in front of them all. And so I sat, and watched, wanting to join in but quite unable to. Poor Mother, how she cajoled and threatened and must have felt so embarrassed herself. And how exasperated she was when, at some time during the week following, she found me trying to copy what I had seen the other children doing, not very well, but very determinedly, in the ballet shoes with which I had a love-hate relationship, for they hurt my toes though I loved the look of them.

Anyway, she must have persevered for I

remember later on enjoying those classes, particularly the summer ones in Miss Butcher's garden, when we all wore moss-green shantung shifts with smocking on the shoulders and a green cord round the waist. Needless to say, it was Miss Twitchett who made mine. Come to think of it, they weren't far off the style we made for our tiny celluloid dolls, apart from the smocking and having side seams.

Into town!

Sometimes on Friday afternoons, Mother and I would take the bus or train to Haverhill. There we might have our hair cut by Mr Ransome on the High Street, and then go and have the most tasty ham sandwiches in the world in the small tea room off Mr Ashard's shop. It was narrow and panelled, and there we sat with a pot of tea and a plate of those sandwiches. Nothing had ever tasted quite like them before, or has since, with just the right amount of butter and mustard on the bread, and the ham so delicious. Such a very special treat, they were.

After that we might go to The Pictures, if there was a Fred Astaire and Ginger Rogers film showing. *That* was another special treat which I devoured with equal intensity, watching their feet, their movements, and how her dress flowed to and fro, and how their dance and the music fitted so beautifully together.

'Are you enjoying it?' Mother would say.

Oh! what an interruption! I could only nod intensely, willing her not to utter another word ever again until it was all finished.

Then we might take another bus, or even be picked up and taken to Steeple Bumpstead to Auntie Mary Humphrey and all her large family for the evening and night. So many of them, and all strangers, even though kind. I could never remember who was which, and felt so small and unable to communicate. John, with the curly hair, was nearest to my age, but he was a boy and not one I played with like at home. Sometimes Uncle Bertie would be there too, and it was all very grown-up, and wasn't home. There was always a kindly hot-water bottle in my little bed, but I did feel homesick.

But back home again there would be the buds on the chestnut trees like always, as dark and shiny and sticky as Hot Cross Buns. And the flattened shiny grass of spring, and the indigo clouds and brilliant rainbows, the familiar, ever renewed coming of things, the pattern always re-established. I loved living in my nutshell, for it was a whole, wide world.

Brownies

Miss Dean's house was at the top of Church Street, set back in the bend of the road, and as you went through the gates the first things you saw were neat, low, clipped box hedges making a pattern in front of the lawn. The lawn was big and long, and at the far end there was a crumbling tower which, as the years went by, became more and more out of bounds. It was like a very small piece of real castle, just our size, with a staircase and windows as you went up. There was more garden beyond, leading down to the river which came from Poslingford.

Our Brownie group always met in the Summer House on the right of the path as you walked down from the house. It held faded canvas chairs, and smelt faintly fusty, but had stools on which we sat in a circle round our Brown Owl. Two-thirty was the time of our meetings, and we were always in uniform, of course, even our Brown Owl, who spoke very quietly, solemnly and slowly. We began by saying all together what as Brownies we promised to do, and what happened after that I can't remember. Except, of course, the books we were allowed to search through and borrow. I kept one called 'The Wallypug of Why' for a very long time, finding that I liked the title more than the book, which I never finished. Gradually we moved to Angela Brazil, of which there were quite a few, but that was later.

What was really exciting were the summer events, when out of boxes came things to dress up in. Muslin sewn on to wire loops and attached to the back of you with safety pins transformed you immediately into a fairy, and you were quite a different being all of a sudden. There were muslin skirts, too, all floaty, just made for dancing in. And most wonderful of all, to make it all quite certain, there were wreaths to wear on our heads. If there weren't enough then we made daisy chains to do the job, and of course they became just as magical because Brown Owl treated them exactly the same as the wreaths. Then we were told to form a circle and dance a story already explained to us.

Bliss. Except that we couldn't all agree...

Every Christmas, Miss Dean gave a party for all her charges, and it was always rather different from going to parties anywhere else. First of all, you felt she was in charge, rather like a teacher in school, and what happened didn't just happen, it was planned. If pencils were needed there was always the right number, and you just knew that everything would work. It flowed. After some games to begin with came tea, which was served on a long table in what might have been the kitchen by a woman called Blanche, who lived with Miss Dean and her mother.

After tea there were more games until at last the most exciting game of all was announced – the Treasure Hunt. This was what we remembered best from year to year, for it led us into all sorts of places, even upstairs, and it was all so different from our own homes. My particular love was the dappled rocking horse that stood by a window on the landing, so beautiful I did not dare to touch it. And each year it was there.

When the Treasure Hunt was over – I don't think I ever won – so was the party. Mothers would come to collect us and take us home. But one thing still had to be done, and that was to be given a present off the Christmas Tree. There were nearly always shiny painted pencils with points sharpened to delicate cones. We loved, too, the tiny net Christmas stockings filled with whistles and other surprises, to be unpacked at home. And pink and white sugar mice with little eyes and long string tails. We took our treasures home, stuffed with happiness until the next year.

The Outing

Once a year it was time again for the Sunday School Outing. We all gathered in unusually large numbers on the Station platform, the

Vicar in unaccustomed jacket and trousers and a Panama hat, Miss Wiffen looking just like her usual self, and Mothers holding some of the youngest hands of the wriggling group while keeping an eye on some of the most wriggly. Painted buckets and wooden spades had been found at the backs of cupboards; bathing suits and sun-hats (depending on the weather) and rubber paddling shoes were packed in shopping bags together with towels and calamine lotion and flasks of tea or orange drink, a rug to sit on and knitting for mothers. Oh – perhaps a painted paper sunshade, too, and even a camera remembered at the last minute. The train came in from Haverhill, we all got in, and off we went for a day at the seaside, miles and miles and miles away, stopping at every station, wondering which would be ours, and how much further it would be.

After what seemed an age, the train would come to the end of the line and out we'd get with all our belongings clutched tightly (or hopefully so) to us. On the pavement we'd pass lots of shops with postcards and sticks of rock and yet more buckets and spades and rubber paddling shoes and sun-hats and brightly patterned balls. 'Come on!' Mother would say. Very soon, with the smell of the sea air in our noses, and floating along with excitement, we'd all of a sudden catch sight of the sea – and then it was a race to find (and it wasn't always possible) a good patch of empty sand on which to sit and build sand castles, just close enough to the sea to fetch water for the moat, and near enough so that our mothers could easily watch us in the waves. Occasionally it could be quite warm, but I vividly remember shivering as Mother towelled me dry, and how nice it was to have a warm jersey on top afterwards.

School

There was a 'babies' class in our school, and that is where we went at three or four. In winter, I remember being rugged up so much that I could hardly bend. On top of shoes and socks came knitted leggings that went up to one's waist, and were held in place below by elastic under the shoe. Then a coat with (of course) gloves on a tape threaded through the sleeves, and on top of that a woolly scarf that came and crossed over in front and was tied behind, and finally a woolly hat. Sometimes I had to wear leather leggings, and Bessie did them up with a small button-hook. Later on I managed to do it too, and then she or Mother would walk me to school.

The first class I remember well was Mrs Moore's. She was the wife of the Headmaster, a comfortable, homely woman who cooked pancakes for us in the classroom on Pancake Day, crunchy with sugar, sharp with juice, tangy with singe. There was an open fireplace with a big guard around it. Four of us sat at each table, on little chairs with embroidered bags hanging on the back. The black piano which Mrs Moore played when we sang the morning hymn, or sang songs, also had an embroidered cloth hanging down its back.

At mid-morning, muffled up in our coats, we went round to the back for our mugs of Horlicks, with nursery rhyme characters on each one. In summer, we had a third of a pint of milk in a bottle with a straw. At playtime the girls and the boys were segregated, and we played ball or made circles and played singing games like 'The farmer's in his Den' or 'Here we go round the sun, here we go round the moon, here we go round the chimney pots on a Su-u-unday a-a-fternoon.' Then there was 'Poor Sally lies a-weeping', 'In and out the windows', 'A tisket, a tasket' and 'Here we come gathering nuts in May'. Then there were the skipping games with their own songs. Once out of school, after tea, in the empty streets, we could spin our wooden tops as well. All you needed was a top, and a piece of string with a knot in the end tied onto a stick about fifteen inches long.

Mr Moore, when we were older, gave us Drawing Lessons. It was a kind of agony, for one's pencils had to be sharp, you had to remember your ruler, and you had to measure accurately. On the blackboard would be a chalk picture which he himself had copied from somewhere – the one I remember was of palm trees and a pyramid – and while walking up and down in his neat three-piece suit he would tell us how many inches we had to measure in from the side, down from the top, and up from the bottom. Waiting anxiously to borrow a rubber before he got to me was another agony, for he would measure with his own ruler and belittle us if we made mistakes. To me it was the equivalent of a terrifying Maths lesson later on in life. I dreaded those lessons. But I still have a small coloured chalk drawing of a parrot which I did happily in Mrs Moore's class when I was five. After Mrs Moore's class you went to Miss Buckle, who was young, and then of course one went to Miss Ager and that was quite a different kettle of fish. There one learned a great deal, and liked it. Dorie and I and one or two others escaped having Mr Moore as our class teacher, except for drawing, for, thanks to Miss Ager, we got to the High School in Sudbury when we were ten. Others were just as able, but it could be that the need to get into a steady job at fourteen was of more urgency than a prolonged education. In those days, choices were fairly clear-cut, for the memories of the Depression were not yet ended and war was imminent.

We caught nits, of course, and the odd flea, but mothers dealt with that with special combs and frantic bed-searches with a piece of wet soap and a lot of palaver until clean sheets could be put on again. When one would almost *listen* for a flea that got away, and so could almost imagine that there *was* one. I seem to remember that happening in a Lowestoft boarding house one year. Keating's flea powder was a last resort, but made one feel unpleasantly powdery. Not that Mother would have actually brought the Keating's in her suitcase, but I think she did after that.

Mother's School

Mother went to school until the age of 13, but not in *my* school, in *her* school, and that was just the other side of Church Farm. I imagine it was behind Mr Sargent's shoe-mending workroom, or in that area anyway. A Mrs Newby was the teacher and there Mother went with a handful of other pupils. But not every day, it seems. For when full of the devil – which she was at times – or from a dislike of the lessons, instead of going a few yards further she'd open the Cemetery gates, slip inside, and be off for the whole morning, right up to the very top of the Cemetery and sit there and listen to the quarter hours being struck. When it was time, she'd let herself out and go home for dinner. But of course you can only go so far for just so long, and she received at least one good hiding from her father. The thing she remembered most vividly about the school was the way the boys on the benches behind would whirl the dead rats they'd caught round the girls' heads. Mrs Newby had a few problems, it seems.

On other occasions, when the sound of the Hurdy-gurdy man's music reached her ears, off she'd be before you knew it, dancing in the street and driving Grandad past distraction. This was probably after she'd left school and was helping at home, but was still child enough to tie the apron-strings of two men in the bakehouse together without them knowing...

The Seasons

Winter

What we did, where we went, depended on the seasons. In winter we played a lot indoors, usually at Dorie's house. One of our favourite games was the 'families' we cut out from the clothes catalogues that came round crammed with small black and white drawings of fathers, mothers and children. From small beginnings the mothers and fathers soon had fifteen children or more and stayed smiling calmly as we walked them with cut-out prams across the tablecloth. Each child was, of course, given a name that had to suit it, and in each one we cut out, unable to resist it, we must have seen something that attracted us. I wonder what it was. The families lived in shoe boxes and came out again the next wet day we were in the mood.

Then, of course, we had schools, even one for the cut-out-catalogue families which took up far less room than the other kind where the pupils were our dolls, from quite big to the smallest, tiniest celluloid one, with perhaps a toy dog thrown in to make up the number to about seven each. At some point we had a phase of making our own dolls from cast-off stockings, stuffed with kapok, with wool hair sewn on at a centre parting only, and then tied with ribbon or made into pigtails. Their characters were extraordinary, and developed of themselves like the colours in the Magic Painting books. We knitted for our dolls, and later on for ourselves, scarves mainly, and then made presents for our families. We also embroidered and had board games, card games, puzzles and scrap books.

But we did not always play indoors in winter. 'It's all iced over down by the Bailey,' someone would say, and off we'd be. Some of my cousins might be there, Ralph Pryke would be there, and Betty Lee and Clarence Rogers and Peter Mayle. And so would lots of others, and we'd all set to making at least *one* long slide, the longer the better and the glassier the better, for then it would be really fast. If the ice was good we might even make two. You had to run up to it a bit like a cricketer about to bowl, turn slightly sideways as one foot went in front of the other, and balance with your arms. And the more you did it, the looser you got and the faster and faster you went. We loved it, and spent what seemed hours at it until the surface changed and it was no longer any use. Yes, we had a few bruises, but it was glorious fun. We quite forgot that the ice became the water where, later on, we'd gather our frogs' jelly in jam-jars, and see newts.

And then came the floods. We in the shop would be among the first to hear that 'it was all out over the meadows and The Holms, and you can't get round by the Priory without you take to the bank there...' 'Don't you go near the floods,' they'd say to us.

Water would be up to the little dock down Malting Lane, and the metal bridge would be only a foot or so above the brown swirling current. Part of the path round The Holms would be well under, and for a dare we had to walk sideways along the post and wire fence keeping just above the brown water sliding quickly past us, to reach the dry safety of the gate by the bridge at the end. It was horrible, but we did it.

'Wherever have you been! Just look at you!' Gran would say, dragging us outside, the stiff carpet brush in her hand, and we'd have to think quickly as the bristles caught the backs of our bare knees.

'Cor! Have you seen the cricket meadows?'

No, we hadn't, and off we'd go to see what was happening there. They were under a sheet of shining water, transformed into a great big mirror. Only by peering over the wall could you see where it had come from, by the little whirlpools and swirls that showed where the river from Poslingford ran.

Gradually the excitement faded, and the level of the water sank, leaving debris of sticks and reeds caught in overhanging branches and against bridges and tree-trunks. The water meadows down by the Priory would have had a good soak too, and later would be lush with thick grass and kingcups and buttercups and cuckoo-pint.

Spring

Spring was when the afternoons lengthened into lighter evenings, and when one longed to change early into short socks and get out of the winter clothing. 'Cast ne'er a clout 'til May be out' was often repeated, and we had to bide by it, more or less. Now out would come good, bouncing, rubber balls for wall games like 'sixes and sevens', tops and skipping ropes.

For 'sixes and sevens' you needed a good flat wall, without windows for preference, an even piece of ground in front of it, and no-one inside who could be annoyed. The Lane was perfect. It had all those things, and was quite safe from traffic as well. There, too, we practiced against the wall with our first tennis rackets, and later moved to the end of the slaughterhouse, using the width of the High Street – even when the Youth Club had been given permission to use the tennis courts up the Backside Fields, for sometimes there would be no-one to have a game with, and the wall was the next best thing.

Springtime was also the beginning of playing Cowboys and Indians or hide-and-seek round the town until it was time to go in and get ready for bed. Four or five of us would meet up, and one would stand in one of the Town Hall porches and count up to a hundred, missing a few out sometimes...

We skipped round the streets, for there was hardly any traffic, of course – only the odd car or bicycle – and if there were enough of us (though usually that was only in the school playground) we skipped in a group, all together in a long heavy rope turned by two others. The one who stumbled was 'out', and had to hold the rope. Or we stood in line, and in rhythm to the turning of the big rope, jumped in as the previous girl jumped out, and took turns to do solo stints, all the while chanting, mostly on one note, various rhymes whose meaning was often obscure or made little sense. One went:

'Up in the north, a long way orf,
A donkey had a hacking corf.
What did he have to make him better?'
(getting much quicker) 'Salt, mustard,
vinegar, pepper!'

and then everyone counted the number of

really fast skips you could do before being out.

Then there were flowers to pick. Not a random occupation but a planned foray, for we thought we knew, and tried to keep to ourselves, where the violets grew best. Others no doubt had their best secret places too! And oh, the sharp, sweet smell of them, their stalks so tiny in our fingers. Then home to put them in an empty meat- or fish-paste jar for Gran, their little heads just propped enough to stay up, and their green stalks dangling like legs in the water.

And primroses! That meant The Woods. Going to The Woods meant what seemed to me a very long walk, half a day's journey to the back of beyond, across the railway line, the Mill meadows and the river to Belchamp Road. Then up the hill and along still further until finally, there was the gate and the track across more fields. And there you were. And there they were, unless of course you'd come too early or too late. In which case you tried your luck in the Big Wood, a little way away. But they were not big, wild woods at all really. They just seemed to be so to us then. Home we'd go with the flowers in our baskets and then arrange them in bunches in the inevitable jam-jars, two for us, say, and one for the Betts, and yet one more perhaps for another neighbour. Their pale, flat faces mingled with a few thick-veined leaves glowed on the window sill, giving off such fragrance as to make the journey all worth while. Later came cowslips, whose flowers we sucked for the 'honey', and they were so plentiful that there were always enough left over to put on the graves that we felt were the saddest ones.

The Bailey had other riches. If you went down between the Dumpty Hill and the side of the bank where the shallow hollow was, the ground became a little soggy. But in a few steps it became firm again. On the far side was still, turbid water, where in winter we'd had our slides, but was now clogged with weeds and thick with frogs' spawn. Dorie revelled in picking it up in her hands and putting great globs of it into her jar.

'You're not bringing *that* indoors!' Gran would say.

Also in spring, when the leaves were beginning to break open, we liked to trespass to the top of the Castle. Nobody ever went there as far as we knew, and the board marked 'Private' always looked so old it couldn't be true any more. It stood by the locked gate opposite the engine shed, and was the start of the path that wound round and round the Castle mound to the very top. The fact that the gate was locked added spice to not quite believing the board, and so Dorie and I would always enter with stealth, when no-one in the railway siding was watching, and disappear quickly up the shallow earth steps with their wooden edges to where the steps joined the real path. From our books, we knew it was wrong to crack twigs as we moved.

On the way up, if the spirit moved us, we might make dormouse houses lined with the prettiest green moss we could find, for any wandering dormouse to stumble thankfully across just when it could go no further. That path became fairly peppered with dormouse houses for a couple of years or so, and to find that they were so well-kept only proved what neat, clean animals inhabited them.

From near the top we could pause and see the back sides of houses that we only knew properly from the street front, and it was like seeing the private side of a person – though in fact these back views revealed little other than windows, a door and a garden. But still, it was intriguing to try and guess which back belonged to which front, and so to whom. Sometimes a figure would emerge from the door and give a clue to the house's identity, and we watched him or her put a pair of shoes or boots down; or go and scrape leavings to the chickens; or dip a watering can in a rain butt. It was like watching a slow, rather inconsequential silent film. And yet we found it exciting because nobody knew we were there.

From the very top rose the slanted remains of part of a shell Keep. From beside it, we could just see the church to the north, and beyond the weather cock were fields gently folding into and beyond each other, with their hedges and tall elms criss-crossing and merging until all was very small on the horizon seven or eight miles away. We could see further than anyone else, and what was more we weren't meant to be there at all! It was just a small summit, really, with vegetation encroaching slowly, but that was what made it so beautifully private. There were two or three graves up there, under the remaining section of the Keep wall. From the top there was another way down. A rather slippery slope led to the top of a big stony wall with an old-looking doorway and a wooden door in it. If we had to, we could slip down there, though I never liked doing so, crouching down and hoping to grab onto something to stop me slipping all the way – hopefully nothing thorny, though it often was. Balancing along the ivy-covered wall, we came to another slope going up, and after that there was a tangled and thorny way through nettles to Station Road. Elder branches, with their white cheesy pith, were quite good 'nettle bashers', though.

We tended to be very possessive of the Castle, and rarely went there with other children, though of course they must have gone there too. We liked to feel it was ours.

By Whitsunday the weather had nearly always warmed up, and I was able to wear my favourite hat made of pale straw, with cornflowers, poppies and white daisies round the crown, and white cotton gloves and white ankle socks. And I went to Church either with Mother or Auntie Hilda if she was home, or both. Gone were the dark evenings of the Holy Week lantern slides, and the terribly doleful Green Hill hymn which I liked so much. The Church would have bowls of frothy sheep's parsley and bright flowers from people's gardens; and Miss Stokoe, as always, would be in fine voice at the organ while Mr Wiffen pumped the bellows.

Summer

We spent a lot of time in the Mill meadows, for in summer when we were tired of the Bailey there was the river down by the sluice gates to play in. It was mostly shallow, and the cows and horses came down there for water. All day we would be there, only going home for dinner and being off again with yet another jam-jar, and our nets, and old plimsolls to paddle in, and perhaps some paste sandwiches and a bottle of diluted squash for our tea. With our dresses tucked up into the elastic of our knicker legs, Dorie and I would wade carefully up the river under overhanging trees, where the water was dappled with sunlight and shade, getting to know every hole to avoid, looking for minnows and stickle-backs, and even finding discarded empty mussel shells on the sandy corner at the end. Then we'd wander back again, and see what we could find in the deeper water near the 'waterfall' and bridge. But not too far in, because it looked deep there, though Dorie was always braver than I.

There were bushes on the other bank, opposite where we found the mussel shells, and in those we made our 'house'. And immediately needed to cook in it, of course. But what, what in, and how? Twigs were plentiful, and with a little subterfuge matches could be obtained, and then all we needed apart from nettles and river water was a tin – which, after a day or two, we found. Dorie, being practical, had the job of lighting the fire, our first ever, and we hugged ourselves with glee as our own smoke went up into the air. Then we assembled our nettle soup – not really intending to eat it, mind you – but there we were, intrepid survivors in a wild country (keeping an eye out for any approaching tractor, though, for we had no right to be there at all).

Later on, in the deeper water by the 'waterfall', we taught ourselves to swim, and even I dared to jump in like the others, swinging off an overhanging branch, letting go of the rasping, pleated leaves between my fingers. Goodness knows what was in that water, but we all survived, and then graduated to The Bathing Place by the metal railway bridge beyond Ashen Road, where grown-ups went. Only a few though. I didn't like it. Sitting on the bank, slipping into the water and down into soft mud, fearing to be out of my depth. Occasionally the train to Haverhill would rattle past overhead.

We seemed to spend summer after summer doing these things, and then, later on, Dorie and I fancied that we had found an island on the Mill meadows, all to ourselves. No doubt others felt the same, only we never met anyone else when we were there. It was perfect, small, almost though not quite an island (otherwise how could we have explored it?). It was our Treasure Island, too small to do much with but it was enough to be there, savouring a feeling of secrecy and ownership. There, one day, we watched a heron standing, waiting for fish, but only the once, and he lifted and flew off after a while. The 'island' was really only used for special picnics, and when we had secrets to tell and important things to talk about, and didn't feel like 'doing'. And we were older by then, of course, no longer reading fairy stories but

144

Angela Brazil, and 'Biggles' and 'William'.

Even when we were much older, in our mid-teens, we might decide to go back there for old times' sake, and sit and tell other secrets, and talk of other important things, although it never captivated us again in quite the same way as it had in the beginning.

But summer was spent mainly on the Bailey. Before it became a recreation ground with swings, a see-saw and slide, there were haycocks to jump about in, move around and build into houses. In our sun-tops – made by our mothers from triangles of material, hemmed all round, the top turned down, tape or ribbon to go round our necks and waists and there you were – we'd scratch names with stalks of dry grass or yarrow on each others' backs and have to guess what was written. Or drum with our fingers a tune to be guessed. Then, rolling over, there were clouds to watch and animals and faces and things to see in them: giants and chariots, witches, distant castles, far shores, all rolling slowly by, changing and fading, to be replaced by the next picture. There were special plants with which to play 'Tinker, Tailor, Soldier, Sailor' and find out who you'd marry. A little cheating now and then was ignored.

The Bailey hills are not high, but they were perfect to roll down, and slide down over the bumpy grass, our bottoms sore and glowing; and up we'd go again. And, on the steep sides of the Gun Hill were bushes with bare earth tracks running from top to bottom between them. Crouched double, one had to descend without slipping and sliding into those bushes with the black, spiked thorns on them. You could hold their short, rough stems before deciding how to reach the next support. It was almost on a par with going to the dentist as far as I was concerned, but some days I managed better than others, and some of the others were so agile and fearless it was pure pleasure for them, or so it seemed.

Some children always had to go home for tea. Others, particularly those of large families, brought jam sandwiches as often as they liked. I knew, if I wanted to, I could badger Mother or Gran into letting me have some too. The freedom was glorious. Sometimes some mothers would bring their childrens' tea in baskets. Home-made jam sandwiches in thickly cut white bread, and flasks of tea. Their presence always made it something special, an occasion, and we couldn't throw the crusts away.

The Bailey had the Dumpty Hill as well, and the big tree at the end of one of the long banks. Just down the side slope from it was one of my favourite places: a shallow hollow, a little away from things, but not too much.

Very short birdsfoot trefoil grew there in abundance, with little red streaks on its bright yellow petals.

When all else failed there were always the trains to wait for and wave to as they drew out. The Station was just beyond the Gun Hill and the trains ran from Sudbury one way and Haverhill the other. We had no conception of what lay beyond Haverhill, but knew from the annual Sunday School outing that after a long journey you came to the sea the other way.

But if there was no train coming and no-one was looking we could climb onto the wide wall topped with blueish bricks, or even walk along it. Sooner or later the signal would lift, and daringly we'd jump onto the platform to peer up the dead straight line through the bridge towards Cavendish. A faint suggestion of smoke, then something black, so tiny, so far away that we could afford to relax. We'd look again. Yes! Soon! Nearer and nearer, then obliterated by its own smoke in the tunnel, it appeared again and slowed and creaked to a stop with a great long hiss. As it pulled out it passed the cattle enclosure, the engine shed and the coal tips and curved slightly to the left, crossing the river and disappearing between the trees that grew along the Holms and hid the Priory.

And suddenly the Church clock would

strike, and tell us we'd be late for tea. Up the Station Road we'd run, over the Market Hill, along by the Co-op, up the Almshouse Lane, round the corner, across the road, past the fish shop and...

'Where've *you* been then?' Mr Crick would say, stern behind his glasses.

And, oh, the wasps in the shop, and the heat in the bake-house. The jam puffs with their centres of dark, shining jam surrounded by a twirl of cream. And the jam turnovers, and cream horns, and little coconut-covered madeleines...

Autumn

Blackberrying was not just a one-day affair. It could happen today, where you had discovered marvels the day before, and then again in a few days time when more would be ripe. And then other places would be just coming on. It was a juggling act to catch it all at its best. Off you'd be with the baskets and walking sticks, the ones to fill and the others to bash the nettles with, and the handles to hook down the too-high branches weighed down with ripe fruit. Such a pleasure to find such riches for free, and be talking all the time, straddling the ditches meanwhile and eating a few as you went. And the baskets would be filled higher and higher with the glossy bobbles, and back home we'd go, our work done, the hedges stripped and the sugar ready for jam or the pastry soon to be ready for the pies.

The shortening days limited our activities, or rather, we had to adapt and change our ways. One withdrew indoors, did indoor things, thought 'in-doors', of being warm, and the character of the house altered as it did with each season. The lamp and candle-light, and the whiter light from gently hissing gas mantles, cast a special quality over that time. The oil stove in the quiet, dark shop cast a pattern on the ceiling, and a warm, oily smell around it. Gran and Mother kept a sharp eye out for any sign of smoking, for it could do that at any time unless carefully adjusted.

Early Autumn was dominated by the beginning of the new school year, and a certain apprehension until gradually one found one's feet again. And then, of course, it was crowned by the thought of Christmas at the end of it. But before that, as the days got shorter and began to get cold, we felt like knitting, and this we did with great enthusiasm. We embroidered, too, and began to consider what we could make for presents. Embroidered mats were one thing, but we also liked making calendars which, no doubt thanks to Mr Moore, we copied from snowy scenes we liked. Most of all we preferred painting our own versions of sunset skies behind old houses lying deep in snow, their windows aglow with yellow light, full of warmth, with smoke coming from all the chimneys, and black tree silhouettes nearby. These we turned out painstakingly, sitting at Dorie's table, with our tins of paints and jam-jars of water, with only the sound of our sighs of concentration and the tinkling noise of our brushes being rinsed in the jars, and the singing of the black kettle to keep us company, until the sound of the back door latch being lifted or the front door being opened let us know that it was time to clear away.

During the second or third year of the War we began to knit long khaki scarves for our soldiers, in garter stitch, some straighter-edged than others. The older women made socks for them on four thin steel needles, with neat heels and tapered toes: Dorie was taught to do this by her aunt Nellie. Some also made pairs of gloves. Many is the time we wound balls of wool from skeins stretched between someone's hands, or round the backs of two chairs.

But before the War, early autumn was the time when Gran and Mother reviewed the winter vest situation, and out would come balls of white silk and wool mixture to be turned into long, ribbed vests. Mine in particular had to cover my bottom, and once they had shrunk or I had grown or both, they would be at it, telling me to stand still while they measured them against me to see how much more was needed. A ribbon was threaded through the neck and tied tightly so that I could be draught-proofed, and the sleeves invariably showed under those of any party frock. Oh dear, those vests!

On top of them one wore cotton Liberty Bodices with fleecy insides and down below one had thick cotton knickers, also with fleecy insides. Long woollen socks came up and turned down at the knees, and the bits between them and the knickers had to take their chance in any icy blast. But so did the boys' legs too, for short trousers were the norm for those not yet in their teens. It was only when the High School uniform allowed one to wear black woollen stockings in winter that our legs felt more snug. Then, mothers bought individual suspenders from Mrs Ince's shop in the High Street. These clipped onto the Liberty Bodices, front and back, and fastened onto the stocking tops below. Which meant, in fact, that it was one's shoulders that held the stockings up!

Three things many of us had ladled into us: thick brown extract of malt; cod liver oil; and something called Scott's Emulsion. There was probably a weekly dose of Syrup of Figs as well, just to be sure.

At the first sign of colds, out came the

camphorated oil, and handfuls were rubbed and rubbed into one's chest and back at night. 'There!' Mother would say, quite exhausted, and off I'd be packed to bed with a hot water bottle. I think the grown-ups did that too, so what with bathing only once a week, and not changing clothes all that often, we must have smelt quite delectable, but never noticed a thing.

Sunsets, Moonlight and the Spring Winds

In our early to mid-teens, sunsets, watched from the top of the fields behind the Cemetery, became for us an almost necessary delight. If one on other of us thought there was going to be 'a good one', then we'd call to see if the other had finished her homework (and sometimes we went anyway, promising not to be long), and we'd race to catch it all before it began to fade. We'd sit facing a cornfield, our backs to the hedge, and watch the whole sky change, completely entranced by the colours that turned almost imperceptibly, and the wonder of it all. When it faded, it was like a quiet completion, and we could return home in tranquillity.

Another excitement was moonlight. When we were considered to be old enough our parents allowed us to go out for a short walk

152

in the moonlit streets – but of course we would always go a little further, and take a little longer. Our favourite walk was to go down Nethergate Street, watching the moon slide behind the black lace of the tree branches, casting a silent stillness and soft shadows that gave familiar buildings unfamiliar characters. And as we went, we spoke quietly, or not at all, caught up in the beauty and the strangeness of it all as we left the houses and made for the bridge by the Gatehouse.

There we would lean and watch the moonlight catch a ripple on the black water. Something would drift by, under us. A plop: some night creature awake and foraging. A nearby leaf would suddenly quiver, and then be still. Sometimes we spoke quietly about such intangibles as imagination, or books, or poetry: I know we also talked of the latest boys with whom we had fallen intensely in love – unbeknown to the boys, of course!

After a while, the moon would have cleared the tree tops and a faint, cold damp would begin to rise. A smell of river, of weed, of night-time essence would pervade, and we would shiver slightly and feel it was time to go home.

Nethergate Street would be quite empty in those days. All lay still in the silence cast by the moon's light as we walked back under the chestnut trees. Occasionally, someone would pass by on the other side of the road, like another shadow. Lights would show through bedroom curtains and as we passed there would be muffled going-to-bed noises and we knew we should hurry, even run, but that would have broken the spell. Nevertheless, to save our skins and ensure further such evenings, there were times when we had to do just that.

Yet another excitement was the wind of Spring, which at times swept the sky clean, and at others herded huge masses of white clouds hither and yon, and blew the shining grass sideways. It took charge of our very bodies, and we ran like mad things with it up the hills on the Common, and then down against it, as though it were a tide.

A Week by the Seaside

We – that is, Mother and I – were very lucky before the War because, unlike Grandad and Gran and Uncle Charles, and most others we knew, we went to the seaside for a week's holiday every year. From as early as I can remember, Uncle Bertie took us in a car driven by a man called Billy all the way to Yarmouth or Lowestoft, or Clacton or Felixstowe. Each time, I was car sick, for the leather smelt; or else it was the smell of petrol. Whatever it was, Mother and I felt apprehensive even before we started out, and she put a bag of barley sugar sweets in her handbag because we all believed that helped prevent car sickness. Why we always thought so when it never did, I don't really know.

Apart from the sand (or the pebbles!), and paddling, and meeting other children at the boarding house we stayed in, I remember one year having my first nightie to wear. It was long and yellow, and thereafter kept for 'best', and was just as nice as Mother's, who slept in the same room with me.

There was also a Palm Court where a waiter brought iced cakes and tea in a silver pot, and where there was music played by four people, all in tail coats. They played waltzes which made Mother smile, and gently wave her hand. And they played songs like 'For it's Love makes the World go Round' ... 'It's a Sin to tell a Lie' ... 'When the Poppies bloom again'... and ''Twas on the Isle of Capri that I found her.' One year the young violinist seemed to me the most handsome young man I had ever seen, in his tail coat, so dark and intent and alive. He must have felt my eyes on him, for he turned to me, and smiled. And there and then, I fell immediately in love for the very first time. I never saw him again, though I looked for him in other Palm Courts...

But what was almost best of all was walking in the dark among the gardens strung with lights. 'Hold my hand, and look where you're going,' Mother would say. Look where I was going? I could not look anywhere else, it was all so beautiful: necklaces of golden lights, both high and low, a small bridge outlined by them, all of it going on for ever it seemed. After such magic one could go quite contentedly to bed. And then the week would be over, and it was time for the dreaded drive back, with the leather and barley sugar and kind Billy, who had come all the way to fetch us.

It was Uncle who decided I should wear shorts to play in for the summer. They appeared, khaki ones, but the red and green elastic belt with the tiny silvery snake clasp reconciled me to them, finally. He also insisted that I wear strong brown lace-ups in the winter, and I can still feel Mother's determination that I *should* wear them, as she tied the laces very tightly. They looked just like boys' and so did the khaki shorts, but in the end they and I became one of a piece.

Endings

War

I suppose that the first time Mother and I had a bathroom and inside lavatory was when Uncle Bertie bought the bungalow in Cavendish Lane for us in 1937 or '38. That is where poor Emma fell through the ceiling when cleaning under the roof, into what was, I think, the dining room. But she was unhurt apart from bruises, and mended quicker than the ceiling. The Bungalow wasn't a success, though, for the walls ran with water and drove Mother to distraction, and it never felt like a proper home anyway. Not long afterwards the Agers house became empty and Uncle bought that instead, for £600. It was very handy, because Mother could still help in the shop and let rooms as well, to earn a little money of her own.

At the beginning of the War in 1939 we were suddenly – and willingly – inundated by a surge of 9th Lancers who needed billets. They were generally thought of as 'those poor young devils who need all we can give them.' Just a few people, like Gran, had grave doubts about the rumoured drinking habits of Scots, and quite expected the worst. Dorie's mother and father took in Jock, who was tall and rangy, and who took kindly to their offer of the weekly bath between the range oven and the table, with the clothes horse draped with his towel as a decency screen. It may have been exactly what he was used to at home, and if it wasn't he never said so. And the little family would have retired to visit next door anyway, during his ablutions.

It seemed that there were soldiers living everywhere, and indeed they were. It was like suddenly having lots of big brothers all over the place. They were in empty houses, they were upstairs and downstairs in people's homes, they were here, there, and anywhere you could think of. They were even quartered in the empty Almshouse next to the Church, and one cheeky, smiling fellow always called and waved as we came out on Sunday mornings. His death came as a shock. He was accidentally killed in what should have been a harmless tank manoeuvre, and we missed him.

Very often at night our hitherto quiet streets would be full of the rumble of army lorries going through. And sometimes, taking the same route, huge tanks would edge and grate their way round Mugg's Corner, and then turn slowly round the Bell into Cavendish Lane. Sometimes they seemed endless, these long convoys going off to Goodness-knew-where, and we couldn't sleep for the noise they made, and so got out of bed to sit in the dark and watch them as they passed. In the morning the street corners would bear the white scrape-marks of the tank tracks, and a brick or two might be chipped.

One lot of troops we had – I no longer remember who or what they were – Irish? Scots? – wore kilts, and one day, for some reason, a section of them, dressed very smartly, marched to their bagpipes on the Market Hill. It was a wonderful sight to watch the way they moved, their kilts swinging in unison to the pipes. Then there was a pause, and perhaps for the first time some of us saw the moving dignity of a Slow March stepped to the haunting sadness of a lament for the dead.

Occasionally Mother's and my house would be let out to a high-ranking officer, and then we would move back to the shop, where two soldiers were billeted with us. One slept on a camp bed in the Front Room, and the other slept in Chrissie's, which had been mine. It was the first time I had ever heard of a grown man having drenched sheets night after night, and in the end it became too much for Gran. But the possible – the probable – reasons for it awoke and startled one into another realm of awareness of what those men had to face.

I remember another occasion later on, when back in our own house again we were letting rooms to married Army and Air Force couples. One day there was a long convoy of troops passing through, and I happened to see a soldier crouched in the corner of the room opposite, suddenly and quite un-expectedly shivering all over and crying, so deeply unable to cope. One felt so helpless. Later on again, a Welsh airman who lived with his wife in our house shot himself. I don't think Mother ever knew why. If she did, she never told me. He had such a smooth and seemingly untroubled face.

But the stresses of war had long tentacles, and searched out breaches and fears that maybe peace had papered over. Nowadays we are, perhaps, more aware of how equally vulnerable we all are in our own ways, and it can be that misfortune unites people and enables real communication, compassion and friendship to take place.

I don't remember exactly when the young mens' uniforms changed. They were still khaki, but sort of smarter, and the accent was American in one form or another. With them came the heavy drone of Flying Fortress bombers taking off and coming in to land at Ridgewell, three or four miles away, and those that hadn't got jeeps found bicycles from somewhere or other so that they could visit their local sweetheart, or find one. That wouldn't have been too difficult: they brought a certain glamour to our little old backwater, and many a female heart pumped the faster for their presence, I'm sure.

I used to like sitting by our window and drawing them as they hung about the steps of the Bear and Crown opposite on summer evenings, and once it was highly exciting to watch a real life drama (from a bedroom window, I might add) as a short, dark-haired American with a knife chased another round the streets. Fortunately, someone had called the Military Police who came roaring down from Ridgewell in their jeep and calmly took charge of the situation. It seemed that they were quite used to coping with the rather volatile Hispanic temperament.

Once we children were collected up and taken in a truck off to the Air Base for a party, and the only thing I can remember is how bright all the lights were, and that we were showered, it seemed, with bars of chocolate and something called Spearmint, and how they really wanted us to be happy.

But what was most surprising of all was the news at the end of the war. For pale, quiet, Florence Mugg had found romance and wings, and flown the nest. An airman from Ridgewell – a fellow Plymouth Brother – had whisked her off to be his wife in far-away America, and none of us had ever suspected a thing!

Gran

Sunday mornings when Gran changed before dinner I liked to watch her, and ask to try on her necklaces, and I'd wait while she opened the mirrored middle door of the wardrobe and then look in the shoe-drawer underneath. It was a familiar ritual that happened every Sunday. But I was always a little careful with Gran, not to cross her, for she was not someone to be cajoled like Grandad and Mother and Uncle Charles. With them there were warm tentacles to be found and played with. But with Gran there was a kind of no-man's land. She smiled little, and sadly I never came close enough to her to know or even to begin to understand her.

I didn't realize until I was much older that when Gran died, mother lost her one dear friend, her ally in a harsh world ruled by men. For them I think it was like that. She died on Easter Saturday in 1941, and Mrs Hurry's daughter and her husband took me for the Sunday to their farm where I found the house very grand, and felt overwhelmed by it all. They were very kind to me, but I was still remembering the unusual hush in the house at home. They gave me a salad of lettuce and beet and green peas. I knew lettuce, but had only eaten it with sugar between slices of bread and butter, and not like this, mixed up with beetroot and cold green peas! And I wasn't hungry anyway. The house had a beautiful lawn with a tall pine growing out of it, but I felt far from home.

While Gran was dying I had been taken up to see her, and she lay on her side of the bed, breathing strangely and noisily. She had only been ill for five days. Her eyes were not quite closed, but only white showed between the lids, and her mouth was open like it had been sometimes when she fell asleep in her armchair. She was sixty eight. The lacquered tin in which she kept her necklaces stood on her dressing table. There, too were the little gold safety pins for fixing her lace-topped modesty vests inside the V-necks of her frocks.

Much of the greyness and hardship of her life must surely have sprung or seeped from the mis-match of her and Grandad's personalities. I can only guess that what attraction there had once been between them soon faded, and they then lived their own way, trapped for ever with their three living children and the business. Grandad read avidly, almost whatever came his way (and that was sparse enough), and he loved meeting people. Gran had tummy pains, and got tired easily, although in their young days they had been great dancers, both of them. But somewhere along the way, Gran had dropped out, and Grandad met people in the pub.

Grandad

The older Grandad got the more of a Village Elder he became – at least in The Bell or The Swan, where in each case he had his own chair, practically out of bounds to anyone else. He liked nothing better than seeing a new face and getting into conversation, or getting together with his mates. A stranger was a cause for celebration, and another glass, and all of that often led him into trouble back home.

I remember a man coming into the Shop, stroking his moustache and asking 'where was Freddie last night, then?'

'How should I know?' said Gran. 'He was late, that I do know!'

It was the day when the new Recreation Ground for children, on part of the Bailey, was to be opened officially. But it seemed that it had been unofficially opened the night before, by the light of the moon. Six figures had been seen sliding down the slide, and having a go on the swings and see-saws, and among them were thought to be the station master's chief clerk and old George, who farmed and at 70-odd was still spry on a bicycle. Who the others were was a mystery, except that those two had been Grandad's cribbage mates for the last umpteen years up to, and including, last night.

'Humph!' said Gran. She had heard quite enough.

People, and books and a drink and keeping the business ticking over were his life. But he didn't keep the business ticking over, and it was Mother, the wilful, mischievous child who (she claimed) he had hit many a time, who paid the flour bills and the corn merchants from her own small savings, time and again.

Sometimes, lying awake in the big bed, I would hear raised voices downstairs, bitter voices, particularly Mother's, but I had my own world to withdraw into then. What went on I was able to make fuzzy and distant, like thick grey cotton wool in another room, and eventually a sort of calm would settle down again. I was not going to enter that room if I could help it, for I was afraid of what I might find. It was their world, not mine, and it was never very long before Grandad came back into my world with me again.

At the end of the War things went badly downhill with Grandad's business. Even today, I don't know all the ins and outs of it. I suspect that part of it was that Uncle Vic, his elder son, was preoccupied with his large family and already weakened by the illness that ended his life at the age of 57. Uncle Charles had no head for business: in fact he moved away to Lowestoft around that time, finding not only work but a kindly widow who was willing to marry him. By now Grandad himself was well into his seventies. Mother, who carried as much of the burden as she could, had a right, I suppose, to be critical. I could not defend him, yet I could not bear the angry words used against him. One day I went to see him, and he was all alone in the Living Room in Gran's old chair. The room was much barer than I had ever known it. The whole house was becoming emptier and emptier. 'I managed to sell my watch today,' he said, and a great big cry went up inside me – for shame, for pity, and also for love of him. But we sat there quite calmly, he and I, and somehow I took comfort in his quiet acceptance of what was happening. And I know I didn't care what anyone else thought of him. He was Grandad, and I loved him.

A little later he came to live with Mother and me in an uneasy truce, with me in the middle. Sometimes we'd take a walk up the Cemetery, he and I, and sit in the porch opposite Gran's grave, and once he said, as we sat in silence: 'Life is really very simple.' I didn't ask him what he meant, for without words I understood. It was sitting there with him once of an evening that I thought of *him* dying one day, and how it would happen, and I thought I knew, for I could see it. Death would come for him out of a pale green sky at sunset, a solitary bird winging from afar, swift and low over the fields, coming for him alone, to pierce his heart with peace.

I told no-one, and kept my secret to be a little magic spell for him.

When he was really old, and not working any more, he liked to sit on a seat under one of the hills on the Bailey and watch the children playing. He loved children and they seemed to love him too, for they came up and sat and talked with him, and brought him button-holes, and he looked after their coats for them. He knew them all by name, and he knew their parents and their grandparents too, and it amused him to sit there and watch their funny ways. He was very content.

This was after Mother and I had left Clare in 1948, and Aunt Cis and Uncle Vic had taken him into their small home, where he was surrounded by the comings and goings and company of the young family. This must have been very much to his liking, I think, and kept his eyes and ears occupied and his mind busy reckoning how to snatch a little reading time into the bargain!

Epilogue

On June 20th 1956, I wrote an entry in the diary I was keeping for my first son, Robert, who was then 6 weeks old.

'This is a sad day. Your great grandfather Pashler is dying and Grandmother has gone to Clare to sit with him tonight. Last Sunday he had a stroke which paralysed his legs and made it hard for him to talk, and he was not able to swallow anything. On Monday you, Grandmother and I went to see him, and he was pleased to see you and gave you a kiss. Then Grandmother fed you while I sat and talked with him nearly all the afternoon.'

The day I last saw him the sky was dull, and Clare was overgrown with bushes and nettles and weeds, and the river looked like a jungle river, dark, stagnant and smelling of meadow-sweet flowers. The air was soft, and the Castle wall looked still and silent standing on its hilltop. The Station was deserted and quiet once the train had pulled out. The day consisted of the Station, my aunt's house, and the Station again. The house had a subdued atmosphere, and everyone talked about 'him'.

'Was that him calling?' 'Is he all right?' 'Leave the door ajar.' 'He can hear what we say, you know.'

I had come because I had always loved him. And now he lay there old, bedraggled, and wistful, but he was not one to complain. When I went to him he spoke of outside things, and people, and what a rum do of his this was. I wanted to be very near him and tell him how much I loved him and how I would cherish him always, but I couldn't for fear that he would guess what was in my thoughts. When the others had turned their backs, I touched him and we smiled at each other.

That was the only real moment because for the rest of the time I tried to be cheerful and to amuse him, and we laughed together, but it wasn't the same. When I had smiled at him he paused as though searching for something, and then slowly smiled back at me. I had only smiled at his face, but he had smiled to my heart, sadly, affectionately, but with his old sense of conspiracy, just as in years past – he and I, and the rest of the world.

The afternoon passed quickly and then it was time to go. I left it to the last moment before I kissed him goodbye, and he tried to raise his head and looked round as though he must do something, say something. He looked surprised, and taken unawares and helpless. His eyes were wide and serious as I kissed him again and patted his shoulder and said: 'I will come and see you again, Grandad.'

He didn't say anything and watched me leave the room.

When we left and walked back across the Bailey to catch the train the sky was full of down from the poplar trees, soft, silent feathers drifting like snow.

He died two days later, at evening, peacefully. He was eighty six.

This Large Print Book, for people
who cannot read normal print,
is published under the auspices of

THE ULVERSCROFT FOUNDATION